Nirbhaya

& others who Dared

Nirbhaya
& others who Dared

Kusum Choppra

Vitasta
Let Knowledge Spread

Published by
Renu Kaul Verma
Vitasta Publishing Pvt Ltd
2/15, Ansari Road, Daryaganj,
New Delhi - 110 002
info@vitastapublishing.com

ISBN: 978-93-82711-49-0

First Edition 2014
Second Reprint 2024

MRP ₹399

Typeset by Vitasta Publishing Pvt Ltd
Cover Design by Bella Anderson and Strategies and Smiles
Printed by Vits Press, New Delhi

This is dedicated to
my sons, Mehirr and Jaiinder
who respect women
And
my grandsons, Aditya and Nooh
may they follow in their footsteps

Acknowledgements

This book has a canvas that traverses the country; which makes for a lot of people who have over many years inspired these stories — perforce anonymously.

God bless all of them.

I wish to especially thank Vishwa Srivastava who encouraged me to put together this anthology of the travails of women and their resolution as a tribute to the courageous Nirbhaya.

Many friends — Bella, Chintan Pandya, Esther David, Gauri, Hrim, Minal Bhatt, Nikita Dudani, Ranjani Shastri, Shweta Parikh and others have helped in this journey; along with my sons, Mehirr, Jaiinder and Pitamber, and my daughters Hemangini, Kaajal, Amina, Karrishma and Muskaan who contributed much more than just their support for Ma.

Not the least, the Vitasta team of Renu, Veena, Alok, Megha and the rest who did the painstaking work of readying the book for bookshelves and readers.

Contents

A New Story

The police siren wailed through the gate and turned round the corner to stop at a small crowd that parted for the *policewallahs*. It was a gruesome sight. The head of the fallen man had smashed on the side of the raised flower bed which was smeared around, part black, part grey and part blood. The rest of the body resembled an elongated balloon.

Someone pointed up. Following the finger twelve floors up, Inspector Jadav saw a frail-looking white face almost tilting forward too. He waved her back frantically.

"Peeche, peeche," he roared. Leaving some men to work with a camera and a body bag, he led the others swiftly upstairs. The 'estate manager' of the society was importantly holding back the curious at the open door to the top floor flat. A scared looking servant was swinging his head from the

crowd at the open door to the frail figure on the open terrace, now in a neat heap, her dupatta clutched in her hands.

"We have rung up their son," offered the estate manager.

The servant added helpfully, "*Bhaiyaji* is on his way…"

Jadav walked out onto the terrace, quietly taking in the setting. It was a well appointed one, with *jharokha* style *jhalis* shutting away the ugly sight of the building's tanks. One corner had a low sitting arrangement in stone, with a lone high cane chair. The rest of the terrace was a garden, the lawn bordered with crotons and just one dash of colour amongst the variegated greens. The old lady was at the far end of the terrace, her eyes wide and huge in her frail face.

Jadav tapped her shoulder reassuringly. She cringed at his touch. He beckoned the servant to bring her indoors. But she resisted his touch too, shaking it off violently. Someone brought a glass of water and held it to her lips. She drank thirstily, and then replaced her dupatta on her face, the blank questioning look back in her eyes.

"*Maaji, chaliye,* come inside." Jadav's tone was sympathetic. Her face became a question mark. *Yahan nahi baithna hai. Andar chaliye. (Maaji,* don't sit here. Let's go inside).

As she remained sitting still, Jadav motioned one of his men to stand guard and moved back inside to question the servant. "What happened?"

"*Saab*, I don't know what was being said, I was in the

kitchen. When I heard the shouting, I came to look. *Saab* was shouting like he always does, his face red and his teeth clenched. He makes huge angry eyes. It's a very scary look…"

"What happened?"

"Then he started walking back towards the house…"

"Where was he first?"

"They were both standing at the end of the terrace and started fighting as usual. Then he started walking back. Then…" He looked a bit scared as there was a stirring at the door. A young man stepped in. *"Bhaiyaji…"*

His face was pale and strained as Rahul walked up to shake hands with Jadav; over his shoulder he questioned the servant, "Bholu, how is Ma?"

Jadav put a firm hand on his shoulder, "Sorry son; your father is no more."

"Ma?" Jadav led him two steps forward pointing to the crouched figure of the old lady. Rahul ran swiftly to her. Putting his arms around her, he almost hauled her up and held her firmly close to his chest, as if imparting his own strength to her. His eyes were wet; hers were strangely dry as he led her gently in. He tried to lead her to the sofa but she nudged him towards her bedroom. Jadav gave a gentle frown. The son firmly placed the old woman in her chair and sat at her feet, holding her hands as he faced the inspector.

"What happened?"

"We were just trying to get it out of the servant. He

says they were at the far end of the terrace and your father walked back into the house shouting."

"*Saab*, he did not reach inside the house. *Maaji* said something to him. Then he stopped and he turned around and shouted loudly, 'I'll kill you'. He rushed towards her with his arms outstretched. I thought he was going to push her off the terrace." As he spoke, he looked straight into the old woman's eyes. The inspector followed the look to meet the strange blank questioning look on the old lady's face.

"Then what happened?"

"*Pata nahin saab* (I don't know), what happened? How it happened? One moment, *Maaji* was standing at that wall and *Saab* was rushing towards her with his arms stretched out and hands spread like this..." He stretched out his fingers dramatically. "Then suddenly…she was down, like you found her… and he was over that wall, still shouting…."

The old lady began to shiver violently but there was not a sound from her lips still under her dupatta, nor a tear on her face. Her son got up, fetched a dash of brandy with water in a glass and made her drink it. He held her close.

"Ma, I am there…"

Jadav was looking on curiously. There was something strange here. The young man's face was pale and strained, almost wary? There was little grief evident. Perhaps the old woman was in total shock. That was a bit worrisome.

His mobile buzzed. "Shake her out of it man," he

snapped at the younger man. "I'll be back in a while," he said as he strode off to the lift.

Downstairs, he encountered the usual gaggle of curious onlookers. His man led an elderly man forward, "*Saab*, he says he saw it happen. He lives in the opposite block and was on his terrace too."

"They usually stand there and argue. It happened today also. He was really mad about something and started to walk back to the house. Suddenly, he turned around and raised his arms...."

The inspector interrupted him, "Yes, yes, I know all about that. But how did he fall? The wall is not that short that he could trip over it. You live there, you should know."

"That is what I have been wondering about. How did he fall? But I saw him fall with these very eyes."

"Did you know them personally?"

When he replied in the negative, Jadav instructed his man to take his name, story and details and strode towards the spot where the body had landed. The stone flooring precluded any chance of survival. He turned to the others, asking if anyone knew them personally. He encountered blank faces. No one wanted to get involved with the police. They all stepped back.

"Look, we are not going to book you or anything. I just want to know more about them. Do any of you know them personally?" Hesitation flashed across a couple of old faces, then the shutters came down firmly and the crowd began to disperse, albeit reluctantly as a wave of curiosity had overcome them all.

The frustrated inspector went back upstairs. He harangued the servant who was unable to say more than what he had said earlier. The old woman was still awake, though comatose. "Call a doctor," he instructed her son as he strode out onto the terrace. The old woman's eyes followed him.

He walked the length of the terrace his arms outstretched, to where he had found the old woman; and reached the end of the terrace. Where the wall met the floor, a strategic curve was in place to prevent just such a mishap. He stepped back and walked quickly forward again. His feet were stopped by the curve. How the hell did the old man fall off?

Jadav walked back into the house. Rahul had taken his mother to her bedroom, still blank, the servant frightened and the son tense. He shot off a stream of questions. How old was the father? How tall was he? Strong? Why did they fight? "What are you looking for, Jadav?" Rahul's tone was becoming belligerent.

"It is plain and simple. No one can just fall off that terrace. How did your father fly off?" The old woman gave an involuntary shiver. Rahul gestured to her, "Can we save this question for later? Our doctor is on his way."

Soon after, the case was closed reluctantly for lack of evidence and a nod from higher up.

As Jadav walked around the retirement home and encountered some of the residents, a recollection of a seemingly familiar face evoked the old memories. The face of the old woman with the dupatta across her face floated before his eyes, somewhat at odds with the serenity on the round face of the old woman who sat at her ease in the circle at the river side.

Jadav joined the group. A short rotund fellow was boasting of his exploits. "Aah…it was such a wonderful feeling. Seeing a princess high above in her balcony with that voluptuous backside drove me crazy the whole day. When the lips on the face were such perfect lotuses, how much more smooth and perfect would those underneath be? Later that night I climbed up the pipe into her bedroom. Perhaps she had seen me… I was a handsome bugger then, no pot belly and extra flesh. She was sleeping without a stitch on, as if waiting for me to come and taste her two sets of luscious lotus lips, enough to drive any man crazy." He went into an indecent description of his seduction before ending with a wild, "I left my mark on her, a huge red stick-on bindi on her ample butt…" He signed off to a roar of raucous laughter, not noticing a shaky hand move wonderingly, tenderly.

Engrossed in the tale of the crude fellow, she did not notice the sharp look directed her way by Jadav, intrigued by the face but not quite able to place it. Staring hard at the stocky boaster, the old lady brought her other hand up with the dupatta to cover the 'o' of her mouth.

The gesture clicked in the mind of the old policeman. His mind went right back to that tall tower with its victim's brains splashed over a concrete edged flower bed and the woman peeping over the top of the terrace.

A chair was pushed back harshly as another woman in the resident group stood up, disgust writ large on her face. "Why do these people tell such atrocious lies? For what? For whom? I don't want to hear any more of this oaf's nonsense." As she stalked off, she was joined by the other women in her group, including the old lady Jadav had been staring at.

There was an easy camaraderie between the two women. Jadav wondered at it — the old woman who went into a traumatic shock and lost her voice at the death of her husband and the other one, obviously a retired professional, woman-about-town. What could they have in common? To facilitate the stalking, he signed up for a week's guest stay, spending more time eavesdropping than checking out what the retirement home actually had to offer.

But the elderly duo were difficult to listen to; they spoke in low voices, often breaking out in smiles and giggles, clasping each other's hands, often away from the main body of residents, male and female. Jadav sought to pick the brains of the manager over a tankard of beer. "Those two ladies seem to be very close. Did they come here together?"

"Not at all. Old Mrs Khanna came here almost a decade

ago. She was very morose when she came, months after she lost her husband. She hardly spoke at all, just hid herself behind her dupatta. We had to work hard at bringing her out of her shell. Even her son's visits did little. It was only when Dr Jayshree came, that the walls she had surrounded herself with began to crack. Even so it took a long time to integrate her in the community, other than her chosen friend."

"What was the common factor?"

"Who knows? Widowhood I guess."

"Widowhood? There must be several of them here. What binds these two?"

"Well, I would not hazard a guess. My wife used to say that widowhood is a tricky business. Everyone talks of the loneliness of widowers and the sorrow of widows, lost without their husbands. What of those widows who finally breathe free after their spouses leave them or the relief of widows who finally get to do something that they wish to do, without a dominating husband breathing down their necks? So you see, it is difficult for any lay person to say why two people are drawn to each other; it is all very personal."

"Where did the doctor come from? Any childhood link, perhaps?"

"Not that I know of Dr Jayshree and her husband were the ideal doctor pair, surgeon and anesthetist, working together so efficiently that she forgot how to run a household, and when he died, she preferred a retirement home like ours which takes care of all housekeeping."

"Do surgeons die that young? Surprising isn't it to find a doctor dying so young?"

"That is a question mark. Only some doctors are health conscious. Dr Jayshree is, but her husband apparently died of a sudden heart attack, out of the blue. No one can predict those."

Fishing for more information did not yield dividends. Perhaps if his eavesdropping had been more ambitious, Jadav would have learnt more.

"Tell me, when you rubbed your butt when that rascal finished his tale, was it because it evoked old memories? Did your husband do the same?"

"That one would never be so imaginative in giving anyone but himself pleasure. But yes, it did evoke an old memory."

"Of what?"

The old lady eyed her carefully, as if making up her mind whether to tell or not.

"Oh what the hell! how does it matter now, after so many years? That was our honeymoon and I must admit that the hyped lovemaking had been a disappointment. Then one night, there was this stranger who really blew my mind. I almost thanked my husband for sending him to me. Thank god I didn't. I found the bindi on my butt just before hubbie dear came to bed in the wee hours, after his poker game. Since I didn't see his face in the dark, there was never any question of coming up with him in all these years...didn't know who to look for! In any case, that husband of mine would have...." She trembled at the memory of the vile temper.

After a while she continued, "What of you? Any such nocturnal adventures?"

"Do doctors ever have them? The staidness of the profession permeates into our bones and marrow, I think. We used to be so happy-go-lucky. Then the rhythm broke the happiness. It was just work and more work, one more surgery and then one more — and one more. I used to plead with him to stop, to take thing a bit easy. We had no kids to leave our fortune to, so why were we amassing so much money? Not even the prestige of research or any such thing, but he just would not stop. I was bone tired and menopause made it worse."

"That I can well imagine. But he would not ease off?"

"He said being busy would cure it all. Ha! what a great cure. Men can be so dense. I thanked my lucky stars when someone railroaded us into a health check and his heart problem showed up. But no go, as far as easing up was concerned."

"Is that how he died?"

"Partly...."

"Meaning?" The pause was pregnant.

"We were at the farmhouse and my mobile battery was down but I did not charge it hoping for some peace. He never carried a mobile himself. Used mine. He was feeling uneasy; so I just let him rest, instead of making a shindig and carting him off to a hospital right away. He seemed the better for the rest and had some soup for dinner before going to bed unusually early. He said he felt tired. When I went into his bedroom in the morning he was gone. Then the staff made all sorts of noises that the sahib had been unwell but memsahib did not call the ambulance, etc., etc. The media played it up, but eventually the noise died down and I sold out and left."

"Don't the question marks remain?"

"Having won my freedom, am I going to clutter myself with those question marks or the unending surgeries?"

"I feel the same. But some people don't let go. You know that fellow who has come to see the place — he keeps looking at me. He's trying to raise the same questions in my mind, after I put them away ten years ago to seal my freedom."

"Who is he and what did you not do?"

"I did. I picked up the feet of my bastard husband and tipped him over the terrace wall. And that damned policeman kept asking how could he have possibly fallen to his death when the terrace wall was that high? He's been eyeing me since he came. Thank God that rascal's story has distracted him. Wonder if he will let go?"

"Let's make him."

"Can we? How?"

Meal Ticket: Anatomy Of A Divorce

"She never came back to even talk."

"For what? Some more wisecracks?"

"To try and save our marriage?"

"What marriage after you'd filed for divorce?"

"She could have tried...." came out petulantly — almost.

"You forget that was forty years ago. She went with her parents to yours."

"She didn't come to me...."

"After you'd told her you loved me and wanted to marry me?"

"Why must you always take somebody else's side?"

"Look at this rationally. Forty years ago divorce was a huge taboo, which you were forcing her to face. She must have been fed up completely already and so all she saw from your stand was 'escape'. For society's sake, she made some noises and let her parents make a lot more. But she saw escape, believe me...that's why she has stayed so firmly away all this while."

"Escape from what?"

"Do you need it spelt out? Y O U."

"What did I do? I gave her the best that I could."

"Giving the best one can is mutual, you know. She probably gave her best too. But perhaps your best and hers did not gel and you always bring such things home pretty graphically, you know, and repeatedly too."

"So you're saying she hated me."

"Hated is too strong a word for a marriage situation. Probably fed up. That's why she used to take off to her parents' home every now and then, as you used to complain — to repair her own balance. She must have been a pretty different creature there than she was here. Because of the baby, she would have never envisaged a split. In those days women were brainwashed to adjust. When you forced a split on her, she must have thanked her lucky stars that the baby was older then, old enough for her to go out and work."

"I don't believe all this crap. I never tortured that bitch."

"Just like that. Would you like to be made to feel inadequate all the time? To be called a dog or a bastard all day?"

"I don't know why I married you at all? Why?"

"I was your __."

"Huh....?"

"Meal Ticket. That's what. Well paid job, easy emotional prey and now, like her, seeking escape from the daily verbal assaults."

An Officer And A Lady

"What is wrong with all the boys here that you can't marry any of them? *Fauji hain, sherdil jawan hain* (they are army officers and brave too). Take your pick," roared the old man.

"Baoji, keep your voice down please. There are officers all around here," pleaded his daughter Priyani quietly.

"Am I scared of them? What is wrong with a father wanting his daughter married?"

"Did I say I would not? Let me finish my short service stint. I have two years to go yet."

"Who will look at an ex-Fauji woman? Now you have the pick of the field. Then leftovers. What is wrong with that Major Rakesh Chugh who is always at your tail? Tell me?"

Captain Priyani gave her parents an exasperated look and strode out of their guestroom in the MES Bungalow, wishing she had never invited them to visit the station. She had so wanted them to see her new life in the Army, the green Cantonment work places, its elegant messes and the pride in the uniform reflected around.

But the visit had rebounded on her with their obsession to see her 'safely married'. Walking into her mess quarters, she fumed, "How do I get them off my back on this? What safety is there in marriage? Why did they encourage me to join the Army if they just wanted to get me married?"

Captain Sushma Sharma, her batchmate, made soothing noises: "Why don't you tell them about Rahul?"

"Who doesn't look beyond his Sheila? No other female exists on his horizon."

"Come on now, you get along with him pretty good too."

The corners of Priyani's mouth drooped. Rahul! Rahul? The thought of her love for that dashing Captain gnawed at her insides; her heart plunged down into her belly whenever they shared a cup of coffee. Rahul carried on and on about his girlfriend, Sheila, in between asking about her affairs. Priyani had carried a torch for him ever since their training days. Everyone saw it, except Rahul himself. Priyani's lips were sealed. The beautiful Sheila for competition?

Sushma pounced: "Look Priyani, your Baoji is not that wrong. Uniforms are all very well, but marriage doesn't vanish from our lives. The uniform gives us an edge only as long as we wear it. By the time we put it away in five or seven years, we're has-beens and eligible only for the leftovers in the marriage market. If you want Rahul, go for it *yaar;* tell him at least and let him make his choice — that bitch of his or the belle of the battalion. You have to give him the choice."

"I've tried, but just can't say it. How do you say 'I love you' to a guy while he's telling you how crazy he is about someone else. I'm his buddy for God's sake."

A dramatic pause and a single heavy word, "Baoji".

"I can't say it to Rahul."

"Then?"

After a longish pause, Priyani said, "Maybe I'll speak to auntyji, Rahul's mom. She'd come to visit last year, remember?"

800 kms away, the call was a pleasant surprise. The Banerjees had often talked of the lovely Captain so obviously smitten with their darling Rahul, comparing her favourably with Sheila's hopping from lap to lap at parties.

"Hello auntyji, Priyani here. How are you and uncleji?"

"*Bhalo* sweetheart. Tell me, what is happening there? How are all of you?"

"May I say something? Ma, auntyji — I don't know how to say this. I love Rahul but…"

"But what, Priyani? Does he know? Have you told him?"

"I can't say it to him. Please tell him for me," she pleaded. Her heart thudded to a stop. When there was no response… "Are you there auntyji? Please forgive me if I've offended you.

I'm not good enough for you." Priyani stammered brokenly, all the time wondering what had happened to her stern, confident, professional Captain Dutt persona.

"*Arrey*, beti, *ruk, ruk.* Who said you were not good enough? You are too good for that blind idiot of mine."

"Will you tell him?" the gloom switched to fervour until the voice at the other end spoke.

"How I wish I could be matchmaker. We had promised we would not interfere in his life. Now how can I say to him 'drop Sheila and take Priyani?' Would that be fair? But, if you tell him and he asks me, I can push your case wholeheartedly. Speak up dear."

The ball was back in Priyani's court.

"What is wrong with you? With Rajesh?" barked Baoji on his favorite topic. "If you don't want to marry him, tell me whom you want, but I'll not wait till you are 28."

The issue hung fire. Every time Priyani met Rahul, he talked only of Sheila and tried to sell Baoji's scheme of things to Priyani. Seniors, colleagues and the fresh-off-the-train parents of Rajesh combined into a powerful front and in no time at all, marriage negotiations were underway. Priyani's eyes had a haunted look as the wedding loomed large.

She made a desperate call, "Auntyji please, I beg of you speak to him. Otherwise my engagement will happen anytime."

"Beti, how can I?"

"Ask Uncleji to do it please."

Then with the wedding looming large she made a final call, "Auntyji, the wedding is tomorrow. Even now if Rahul says 'yes' I'll go off with him and the hell with everything else."

The two old people exchanged a worried look. Hesitating, stopping and stalling, they dialled his number. "Rahul, beta, how are you?"

"Fine Ma. Remember Captain Priyani? She's getting married tomorrow."

"She's a lovely person. You should have snapped her up yourself. Who is the bridegroom?"

"Ma, Rajesh is a handsome hunk, slightly short-tempered but otherwise a good guy."

"Beta...."

"Bye Ma, I have to go."

The next three days were agony for Priyani. Her eyes followed Rahul as he went about organizing her wedding. The old people saw each detail in their minds' eyes with as much pain as if it was their daughter being married. A fortnight passed uneasily. Things must have settled now, they thought. They usually do, they reasoned.

"Hello, beta, how are things there?"

"Fine. Tell me how are both of you?"

"We are fine. But how is your friend Priyani?"

"Bad show Pa. We all thought the world of Rajesh. He's

a solid drinker and he thrashed Priyani so badly she has had to go on leave to her parents."

Tears seeped out of the closed eyes of the old lady. Her voice was a broken whisper as she spoke to Priyani. "I'm sorry my dear. This is all my fault. I let you down very badly. If only I had had the courage to order him."

"No Ma, please don't blame yourself. It was in my fate; else I would have found the courage myself."

The old woman turned brokenly to the setting sun framed in her window, railing at herself— how could I have been so stupid, such a coward? I could have saved four lives if I had spoken up....

800 kms away, another pair of haunted eyes stared unseeingly at the same sunset, fingering the bump on her scalp from last night's violence.

"When you know he is violent, why did you raise any issue at all?" demanded an unsympathetic Baoji, stodgy in his 'safely married' comfort.

"So you want me to become a dumb cow like Beeji?"

The big eyes flashed red. For the first time in her life, Priyani saw her mother step forward and place a restraining hand on his shoulder. "Why do you say things which will push her onto the divorce road you don't want her to take?"

Baoji looked up in surprise at the first ever rebuke he had got from his wife. As he stood up his hand shot out. Quick as a flash, Priyani shot forward and grabbed the hand. Two pairs of angry eyes crossed wordlessly. Beeji stepped out of range as he turned on his heel, "Book the tickets."

At the station, before Beeji could say her piece, Baoji pronounced, "We do not want a divorce. Things will settle down eventually. Rajesh is not a bad sort."

Priyani pursed her lips. Then she burst out, "How many dumb cows do you want? Aren't you satisfied yet with your 'safely married' rant and what it brought me (she touched her belly) and where it is taking me?"

She marched off leaving a question mark in the old parents' troubled minds. As she walked down the long platform, she heard a muted shout: "I will not live in this Cantonment slum. Get out fast if you want to marry me." Glimpsing Rahul putting Sheila on the train, she slipped off. Later, nursing her drink with Sushma, they listed her options.

"Don't cut off your nose to spite your face, Priyani. Make him suffer too. Think of a way to get out on top of this mess. Don't shriek divorce and turn all these guys against you. They will always stand up for each other and accuse you of 'loose character'. It has been their easiest and most effective cover-up for their mistakes for centuries."

"Then?" both frowned in concentration, discussing their options. "Suppose I apply for a transfer?"

"The CO will ask 'why,' since couples normally want to be posted together. Then they'll go the counselling route;

Rajesh will do the sorry act and then back to square one if he convinces them."

"Suppose I report to the MI Room for medication next time. They'll come to know."

"Why not tell the CO and let Rajesh also be questioned? But how does it get you your freedom?"

"That's the whole point. I want to get away from here. Put some distance between me and this, so I can sort myself out. I need time for that and to plan ahead, even prepare for a career when I get out."

"Wow, that sounds sorted out and reasonable too. What about divorce? Or are you hoping that distance will make him grow fonder?"

"Even if it does, what about those fists? I need the distance to sort myself out. Maybe," she stopped with a sloppy grin, "I'd like to land him a good one and see the shock on his face, maybe just once?"

A giggle burst out of Sushma. "Gory woman. Then what? He'll thrash the daylights out of you."

"Once it is out in the open and I don't need to cover up, you think I can't fix him. What were we trained for? In any case, he'll not do it in public. His reputation is too precious for him."

"Priyani, just think, the trouble is all at your doorstep. What's at his?"

"Why should we constantly think about the men only?

Let him think for himself. I will think only about myself from now on. I want to get out of here, by hook or by crook. Let him face the questions. Now I'm going to fight, for that transfer and an extension to. Once I am ready with another career post-Army, I'll put in my papers too. And lead my life as I want too, without a tyrant tying me down all the time. No more Baoji. And no divorce. Without a divorce, which he is not getting from me— unless he leaves the army, he'll not be able to do this to another woman – hopefully."

"Ameen."

A Daughter's Vengeance

Despite Maya's long-delayed homecoming, dinner was a sombre affair with the children all subdued and Maya herself coping with shock. The children took their places strictly in order of seniority. A servant led a little one down to take her place after Maya's five year old Lekha.

Maya froze when she saw the baby's face, just younger than her Lekha. That face!

White to her lips, Maya injected hostility and accusation in the eyes she turned to her stepmother. For once in her life, Raji's gaze dropped before Maya's.

That was little consolation for a Maya steeped in recalling her strangely abnormal arrival, sans aunts or siblings at the station, the silent, run down *kothi,* Raji's dishevelled appearance and most of all, the shocking change in her beloved Thakurda, the life sucked out of him, so visibly aged, bags under his eyes, shoulders stooped.

'She let Baby's face tell him about her betrayal!' Maya almost convulsed at the thought. 'He knows that he's been betrayed.'

Later she wished she had spent more time with her father that night. As they paced the garden, he had confided: "I wonder what she will do after I am gone." Maya hushed him but he insisted: "I was only waiting to make my peace with you. My time is running out."

"Don't even say such inauspicious things..."

"Maya, all of us have to go. I knew as soon as she said she was pregnant; Vaidji had separated us earlier. She was shameless! What will happen to her after I am gone? And that scoundrel making your and Suman's lives hell."

"Suman?" burst out Maya.

"Yes, her too. My fault; I thought a good family was enough. What will happen to Raji now?"

Maya wondered at the naivety of the love-blinded old man. Could he still not realize what had happened under his nose even with the anguish of his daughters to guide him to his eldest born, lovingly called Dada by all?

Dada had barely waited for the festivities of Suman's wedding to get over before he left home to march into the Army, with no notice to anyone at home.

Then he had stayed firmly away, not willing to betray himself to a stepmother more his contemporary than his father's.

But, immersed in the depths of his own loss, Thakurda did not see or recognize his son's obvious anguish as he continued to moan about his unfaithful wife.

Wordlessly Maya stood up and cradled the massive grey head in her arms and tried to find a lost peace. She never really felt happy or at peace except in the presence of her beloved Thakurda.

True to his word, Thakurda had waited only to see her. That night, he died quietly in his sleep. Looking down at the beloved still form Maya's mute heart wailed: 'Why, Thakurda, Why? You were always so strong. Why did you allow this bastard to weaken you? Why did you not avenge your honour and kill him with your strong bare hands? You would have released me from this heavy lifelong sentence as his wife.'

Later in the day, Maya took a silent vow at her father's bier.

'No more bowing to his tyranny; Dev has destroyed my father; I shall destroy him, whatever sacrifice it may take from me. If it turns me into a shrew, so be it.'

Dada saw her standing deep in thought and raised his eyebrows in query. Later Maya told him everything. Not that he was unaware of the raucous flirtation that Raji had had with her son-in-law, Dev, Maya's husband, during the nuptials of their younger sister, Suman.

Dada himself had been present and in such an emotional churning that it wrung out an unspoken realization. 'I love my mother but not as my mother.'

He left abruptly, before too many persons realized that he carried that torch and was unaware of the aftermath of that flirtation: the birth of Baby Rati, cast in the mould of her father, to announce the betrayal of Thakurda by his young wife and his son-in-law.

"Will you back me now?" Maya demanded.

"Absolutely." There wasn't the slightest hesitation. "What do you want me to do?"

"We could not save Thakurda; but we can save the honour of his memory. Dev has not seen the baby yet. Raji and the little one have to go. No one, especially not Dev, must ever see them here."

Dada was caught off-guard by Maya's demand.

"Where?"

"She always wanted to send her boys abroad. Let her go with them and take the little one also."

"Who'll tell her?"

"You are now the head of the family. You must." The burden Maya put on him was terrible — that of banishing his beloved forever, never to see her again.

"Have you thought of the cost?"

"There's plenty in Thakurda's accounts abroad. If more

is needed, sell something — land, anything. We owe it to Thakurda's honour."

"Maya, Dev is your husband...."

"Leave him to me. I'll take care of that angle," she interrupted grimly. "First we have to ensure that he does not see the little one when he comes now and that he and Raji are never left alone together. Perhaps it may be for the best if the little one is raised away from all the gossip here. Also, don't tell anyone, anyone at all, of our plan, until it is time to tell her to leave."

That was not difficult to achieve. In any case, the children were kept occupied well away from the mourners and the guests. A large number of women mourners hemmed in the widow, away from male eyes.

Dev made a belated entry; Suman not at all!

The funeral was an elaborate backdrop to Maya's memories of her disastrous marriage to Dev.

She had never dreamt that a person could be so narcissistic, that he could actually be evil without knowing that he was being so. Perhaps, she reflected, Dev did know but refused to acknowledge it? That made it easier for what was left of his conscience, even if the accumulated effect had robbed him of his sleep; Dev was a chronic insomniac.

Maya

Consternation showed on many faces when Suman arrived

for Maya's wedding.

She walked in with all her college-practised aplomb and missed the despair creeping into Maya's eyes — conscious now of the inevitable comparisons. Bitter memories of old preyed on her mind.

Suman's beauty and confidence carried her straight into Dev's heart, tickled pink at the appearance of such a stylish sister-in-law. He flirted boldly with her and she responded with glee, flaunting herself all the more to spite the frigid disapproval writ large on the face of every aunt present.

"Won't you invite your sister to go back with us?" Dev asked his bride of a day, with a broad smile.

Maya looked at Suman with barely moving lips. To her consternation, Suman agreed with shameless alacrity and proceeded to fight off all the objections of the aunts, until Thakurda saved the day.

Firmly grasping Suman by the scruff of her fair neck, he pulled her back, "You can go later to meet Maya." The Ides did not seem too favourable for a peaceful marriage; that was proved all too soon when Suman came to visit.

One day, her control snapped and Maya screamed venomously, "You are a shameless prostitute who has come to ruin her sister's home," at the saucy-eyed apparition before her.

There was a loud report — thwack — as a powerful slap almost knocked her head off her shoulders. Maya toppled to the ground sideways, catching a cheek on the wicked edge of the carved table. It left a bleeding gash.

Her younger sister Suman had bent instinctively to help her up but was rudely pulled back by Dev. "Let her be. She can go to Beeji for medication and cold comfort. You come with me."

Maya stood up slowly, gently massaging her wounded cheek and looking at the retreating figures with smouldering eyes.

'That,' she brooded, 'is my little sister and that is Dev, my husband, smitten because she is fresh out of college, clings prettily, speaks English and wears trendy suits, instead of these Victorian lace and ribbon confections foisted on me by his first wife.' Her bosom heaved with heartfelt resentment.

It was not as if Suman was particularly good looking or Maya was bad looking herself. Rather they complemented each other, with a strongly discernible family resemblance.

Tall and angular, Maya was a full head taller than Suman, with rather stern features and an aversion for any sort of reading, a fact that earned her husband's ridicule.

Suman was petite with curves in all the right places. Her stylish high heels and deep slits in her kameezes gave her a swinging, hippy gait which would have turned the head of a saint — which Dev most certainly was not.

In fact, Maya had always secretly felt — secretly because

if she had dared to say so aloud, he would really do something to the contrary just to prove her wrong. Behind his well-cultivated, "hail fellow well met" geniality, he was quite a martinet, with set ways and opinions, to which he was a slave. Those traits only surfaced much later when he was much older. At the time of his marriage to Maya, he was stylishly and self-consciously suave.

That Suman incident had come a few short months after marriage, too early for Maya to have learnt to contend with either Dev's handsomely smiling audacity, or Suman's bravado. Her plea back home had been frenetic and the response immediate. Suman was recalled to be shown off to prospective in-laws.

All three knew that for all his suggestive gestures and talk, Dev would not go beyond bold caresses. Negotiations were already underway for Suman's marriage and which respectable family would accept 'soiled goods', no matter how impeccable the antecedents. Dev himself was the centrepiece of the negotiations as the prospective groom was his cousin's son.

Maya smarted from Dev's blatant flirting with her attractive little sister and the bigger betrayal at home.

It took her days to digest that bitter truth. Dev claimed that Thakurda knew about it. "Why didn't Thakurda or someone else tell me?" Maya wondered.

When she reached her new home, she was received with

all the due rituals by a contingent of elderly ladies. That there was no mother-in-law had been one of the plus points of the match.

Thakurda had gleefully pointed out, "You'll have a proper *Bharat darshan* with a husband in the civil service and no hassles on the home front."

Beeji's hold over the household slowly became evident. Beeji was squat and dumpy, balding with a hairy chin. When she nodded her approval after examining Maya's trousseau and jewellery, everyone almost sighed with relief.

Even Dev deferred to her. She was obviously older than him. Yet not very old. She ordered the servants, decided the menus, the new bride's outfits and all the post-marriage giving and taking.

Maya remembered frowning when Dev had said: "Ask Beeji." That was the first time when she asked for the locker keys to change her bangles. But since Beeji handled all the transactions and the housekeeping, perhaps it made sense to keep the jewellery in her safe.

Beeji seemed to be running the whole show, down to the clothes prepared for her — she recognized the designs of an older generation. Maya had not deemed it fit to question who she was, perhaps a particularly close or favoured relative, whose close ties gave her the right to take decisions, no doubt.

Then everyone started leaving; everyone, except Beeji.

Maya could not even remember how and who told her the bald truth: that Beeji was his first wife, Dev's obligation to an elder brother who died early.

But for the deception which rankled, Maya got along well with Beeji who handled all the chores, leaving the younger woman free to devote herself to building up her marriage. With a wisdom beyond her years, Maya decided to put the humiliation of Dev's wedding day flirtation with Suman behind her, to concentrate on building up a relationship with her husband, of the kind that he had not shared with his first wife.

Tough job, that. At times, he was so easy to get along with; at others, it was as nerve-wracking as walking on eggshells; no-one knew from one moment to another what Dev's reaction would be. She sometimes thought he made a conscious effort to undermine what little confidence she had.

Once he approved of Maya in pale green... "very cool, yes that's it."

The next time he said, "it gives you a TB patient look."

If Maya sat, he would ask, "Must you squat all the time?"

When she stood up, he would laugh, *"Kyon, khade gaon se aayi hai?"* (Have you come from a village where everyone stands?)

If she napped in the afternoon, he would snap at her for wasting time. If she spent the noon making pickles or knitting, he would scold her for not resting herself and not letting others rest. Above all, there was that constant talking and constant carping, that restlessness and emphasis on loyalty, when he was the ultimate betrayer.

He kept his first marriage a secret, never mind if she was a family widow on whom he had been compelled to *chaddar chadao* (marry to offer protection). He should have revealed that detail to Thakurda. She ruled the roost and Maya took all the critical carping.

In company, he "loved" western food but threw tantrums over baked dishes on the table otherwise.

He was in his element in groups, but needed a crutch, a whipping boy to be the butt of all his jokes. Maya sometimes wondered who had played this role earlier. The gregarious social evenings were a prolonged torture that would haunt her for a long time to come, even after they ended — the day after Dada came to visit. The memory of that day was etched in her memory.

"To this day, I wonder how I managed to hang on to my patience and my play-acting of a wife. The Maya, who could whip up 24 types of pickles and 32 different snacks to serve up to his never-ending flow of guests, the Maya who snapped to attention at the sound of Her Master's Voice and jumped to do his bidding at all times and at any time, day or the middle of the night. Whilst I did it all, I simmered with growing resentment and bided my time malevolently," she recalled.

"Dev always said that personal affairs should remain, within the four walls of the house; while he himself cuckolded my father. He exposed his peccadilloes to the whole world at the expense of my Thakurda and his honour." That determined Maya's revenge: that he should never see the face of his beloved again. Every day she prayed for an end to the waiting.

A year passed after Thakurda's death and one day Dada appeared at her doorstep. It was a Sunday and Dev was at home. Maya shot Dada an anxious querying look; his response was reassuring, but she remained nervous. Perhaps that had become a habit. Dev was his usual hearty self.

"How is everyone at home?"

"All's well. I have taken personal charge of everything now..."

"You shouldn't have bothered. I could easily have handled things while you were away on duty...." protested Dev.

"I have already put in my papers. My duty now lies with my family."

Maya knew this, but Dev was stunned; no chance of getting his grubby fingers into Thakurda's pies now. He recovered quickly.

"Raji must be pleased. With such a large establishment, one needs a man about the house."

"She'll soon learn to be a man herself, where she has

gone." Dada was abrupt.

Dev blanched.

"Where has she gone?" he asked sharply.

"I just saw her and the children off. There are better prospects there for Baby too and the children will keep Raji busy between them."

"Who is Baby?" The tone was now distinctly shrill.

Maya held her breath. Dada's reply was painfully careful as he looked into Dev's eyes. "Baby is my youngest sister, born to my stepmother six years ago."

The blood shot into the thin bald head and the black-rimmed glasses could not hide the eyes. Dev caught his breadth audibly; then he blurted out, "Six years ago? Why was I never told of this? How could you just send them away? Who are you to do that?"

A dozen replies chased each other on Maya's eager lips, but Dada quelled them with a look. Drawing himself to his considerable height, his voice took on an unspeakable dignity as he declared: "What interest could you have in my stepsister, when your own daughter had just been born? Besides, at that advanced age, another daughter is not happy news for our parents to celebrate over much. Since my father is no more, the duty of providing for all my younger brothers and sisters devolves on me and I shall always do it as I see best. We decided that, given the circumstances, it was best for the whole family that Baby grow up abroad. Raji will never return to India, at least not until Baby is married — there."

It was out in the open. Maya held her breath, waiting to see if Dev would dare to acknowledge Baby and to challenge Dada.

Even Beeji realized that there was something big going on here. She had heard Dev boast of how he had my stepmother wrapped around his little finger during Suman's nuptials. For once, Beeji watched carefully, her eyes darting from one face to another. At last she caught Maya's eye. Perhaps the hint of triumph gave her the clue she was looking for and the look she gave Dev was triumphantly malicious.

'Ah ha, you're caught in your own mess for once, you rogue', it said wordlessly.

But Dev had collapsed. Maya wondered how much of the collapse was from the weight of the knowledge of a widely known by-blow, the total loss of his prestige in his *sasural* (in-laws house) and how much from the awareness that he was one against three with no relief to be expected for the moment.

It was the end. The sharpened knives were out and there was a whole lifetime in which to turn them. She flung off the mask of the meek little woman.

"How does it concern you anyway?"

The Dev of old turned on her in a flash, but was taken aback by the blaze in her eyes.

"I," said Maya with a distinct emphasis on the 'I', "saw Baby the day Thakurda died." Nothing more needed to be said.

Dada was dangerously icy.

"Look Dev, don't tempt me to kill you and take Maya home permanently. I have come to tell you that I am not Thakurda who quietly suffered your betrayal because of his daughter. As far as I am concerned, you murdered my father. If I ever hear from anyone that Maya has been troubled in any fashion, that will be the last straw. Don't worry, if I can look after your illegitimate daughter, I can take care of my widowed sister and her legitimate daughter as well. Henceforth you will only be tolerated because you are Maya's husband."

The dangerous look in his eyes warned Maya not to say a word more. He stalked out.

Suman's story

It was a let-down. Dev's cousin Ved was handsome, more than Dev, but he had nowhere near his sophistication, nor his charm. He smiled quietly at Dev's naughty jokes but did not contribute. Anyway, the marriage was fixed.

Dev organized it and boasted to Thakurda, "I know him very well. She will be happy." But it was really disappointing.

At the wedding, Dev hardly looked at me or even at Maya in the full glow of early pregnancy. He had come with his strategy for winning hearts mapped out.

He headed straight for Raji. God alone knows what he said to her, from the day he arrived, she tied him to her side. The two were all over the house, billing and cooing; the sisters flushed under the pointed looks of the aunts, but could do little since the silly couple were careful to do so only when Thakurda was out of the house. Who would dare to tell him?

The only time Dev was not with Raji was when either Thakurda or Dada were at home. Something strange was happening to Dada too. All of a sudden, he forgot how to smile. It couldn't be the prospect of losing me — more probably Raji.

Maya's triumphant announcement, "Thakurda will be a grandfather", was blighted by the Dev-Raji flirtation.

Maya and I had caught them red-handed. Maya started, "everyone is talking about you...." but was stopped by a tirade of ridicule from a saucy-eyed Raji.

"She's anxious, not about her husband, or her mother, but about those old crones. Dev, tell her that I'm saving Suman from being ravaged and I'm saving her too; she's in that delicate condition and can't oblige you." Then a parting shot, "Why be jealous when you can't give the man what he wants? And don't go crying to your father; leave him at least in peace."

Who was this hussy? Where was the beautiful stepmother

who had won over our whole large family and twisted Thakurda around her fingers?

The full extent of Dev's treachery was much much deeper, I only discovered too late. My new home was a beautiful, spacious, old-fashioned *haveli,* well maintained with considerable expense and exquisite taste. It was very elegant, compared to the rather casual splendor I was used to at home at Thakurda's. Raji was no lady of the manor.

Dev's presence changed swiftly from the reassurance of familiarity to a shocking trauma of humiliation which continues to send shivers of shame down my spine.

The drinking and partying for the menfolk continued late into the night. I fell asleep on the bed and was awakened by a fumbling hand inside my sari. Fortunately I had been warned and did not panic. But it was uncomfortable, so I decided to keep my eyes closed. As the tears seeped out from the corners of my eyes, I heard a hoarse, "Open them bitch and don't make a noise."

My eyes flew open, widening in shock. Dev was leering wickedly over me

"Hi sweetheart; did you think I'd give you away just like that to this lump?"

He gestured sideways and I turned my head to take in the sight of my brand new husband, drunk as a sod, passed out on the bed. Dev clamped a hand over my mouth. My sari was thrown over my head and I felt a searing pain in my loins. I squirmed to shrug off the invasion but to no avail. It lasted an eternity. Abruptly it stopped. The hand withdrew and I opened my mouth to take in gulps of air. Dev was grinning down at me foolishly. "Great fun; will meet tomorrow." I must have passed out as he started to saunter out of the room.

When I came to, it was morning and Ved was fussing around me. I really thought that I had had a naughty dream. Nevertheless, a sense of terror kept me among the ladies all day.

To my eternal shame, that night too I fell asleep, only to be awakened by a thud as Dev threw Ved on the bed, once again out like a light, to head for my side of the bed, grinning widely.

"Ready?" He asked, raising a sardonic eyebrow. Paralyzed, a part of my brain observed the fluidity with which he repeated the motions of yesterday. It was no dream — the fumbling with his clothes, the hand on my mouth, the sari over my head and then the energetic rocking and pumping and the almost casual, "see you tomorrow."

I lay awake in shock all night. The third night I waited up.

"Did I keep you waiting?" he asked, Ved slung over his shoulder.

"Dev....." that was as far as I got.

"Don't say a single word, just open your legs. It's too late to say anything now; nobody will take your word against mine. Besides," he pointed derisively at the inert Ved, "what can he do? Maybe I'll get you a son. You may live to thank me for it."

I felt soiled and sore. My brain was numb. What could I do? Who could I go to in this household? My languor and red-rimmed eyes made me the butt of sly jokes; no-one guessed.

One night, I kept a vigil, deep in the shadows of the gallery overlooking the hall where the men sat drinking. Dev was plying everyone with drinks, large ones, mixed ones. I jumped when a firm hand descended on my shoulder.

"Bahu?" My eagle-eyed mother-in-law. I turned in terror and then ducked instinctively, hoping Dev had not looked up. *Mataji* followed swiftly. I was mute, but she joined in my vigil. Both of us saw Dev carefully filling glasses and finally furtively tipping a potion from a ring into Ved's glass.

We looked at each other. Wordlessly, she pulled me into my room. A wordless flood of tears later, I confessed. She gave me a quick hug and passed me a glass of water.

"Everything will be alright." Pressing my head onto the pillows, she adjusted the night lamp and sat down in a vast chair in the shadows. We waited.

Dev carried Ved up and threw him on the bed. The old lady spoke, "Thank you Dev, you can go now; I'll help Suman."

If I had not been taut as a string, I would have laughed aloud at the consternation on Dev's face as he swung around.

"Good night Dev," she said firmly as she stood up. He

had no option but to leave quietly. As his footsteps receded, she turned to me, "Lock the door. Nevertheless, I'll be outside."

I sprang to touch her feet in thanksgiving and humility. Rather belatedly relief flooded through me, and as I pulled the latch my knees caved in. I lay against the door for a long time.

The next day was a prolonged cat and mouse game with three players, Mataji, Dev and me. Hats off to the old lady! She unearthed a family hunting lodge in the foothills, had it put into order and packed Ved and me off for that new-fangled fashionable 'honeymoon'!

Before we left, she took me to her suite and pressed a paper into my hand. "This is our phone number. If Dev shows up, call at once."

As we drove in the open family limousine out of the huge gates, onto the open country road, the mists began to clear from my benumbed mind. Slowly Dev receded from my vision and I was able to smile back at Ved. Our idyllic honeymoon lasted all of two days. On the third morning Dev showed up riding his horse right up to our breakfast table set up on the lawn. My stomach pitched.

"Good morning," he smiled. He was his usual self, cracking smutty jokes and jollying up Ved. He took Ved off for a stroll to discuss a hunt.

Taut-faced and shaky-handed, I *dialled Mataji's* number.

It took an agony of suspense to get through to her over the crackling lines. Hearing the returning voices, I had almost replaced the receiver when a voice crackled through, just in the nick of time, "How are you both?" I could hear them coming up the verandah.

Quickly I breathed a single word into the mouthpiece, "Dev" and replaced the handset, turning guiltily as Dev and Ved walked in.

"You look ill, Suman. Isn't Ved looking after you?" Dev commented.

"I'm okay. Have to see to the lunch." I ducked out of the room. My breath remained caught in my throat and I felt like a rat in a trap, watched by a beagle-eyed Dev, who spoke to me all the time through Ved.

Perhaps I only let out my held-back breath late in the evening when a car rolled up the driveway. All three of us rushed out. Ved's parents were climbing out.

"I thought it would be a good idea to come and see how you children are doing," announced the old man grandly. "Dev, what on earth are you doing here?"

Mataji gave me a gentle embrace and wiped away the tears seeping out from under my eyelids.

Since he and the old man got along like a house on fire, Dev was all over us, visiting every few weeks wherever we might be, at the lodge, the *haveli*, Calcutta or Delhi. Out of deference to his relationship with her husband, *Mataji* did not give him any chance to suspect that she was up to his game, jollying him, laughing at his jokes, but sitting in on all the sessions and breaking them up early. "Dev, you have leave, but your *Bhaisaheb* and Ved have to work; off to bed all," she would say in dismissal.

Never knowing when he would turn up gave me spasms of tension in the pit of my stomach. That turned to terror, when the calendar sent me rushing to my mother-in-law. "*Mataji....*" I was unable to articulate, pointing to my stomach.

She grasped my hands firmly. "I was waiting for just this." I turned stricken eyes to her, mutely asking that she understand my plight and that I would not have to speak out my shame.

She looked long and deep into my terrorized eyes and somehow understood. "Dev?" I nodded.

"How many times?" Still dumb, I held up five fingers. Both of us closed our eyes, one in guilt and the other perhaps in sorrow? It could have been her first grandchild! The next morning, *Mataji* announced that she needed some solitude and that she was going up to the lodge. I was to accompany her. Late in the evening, we walked into the nearby village where she sought out the midwife.

Two days later, we slipped into the midwife's house late in the evening. No one saw us. I was shivering with fright in anticipation, of what? The actual pain made me scream;

they stuffed a handkerchief in my mouth.

We stayed at the lodge for over a fortnight. Every day the old lady came to give me a vigorous massage and a piping hot bath. Gradually my numb brain relaxed, my skin and limbs began to glow with her ministrations, the fresh air and the peace.

Mataji took me straight home into Thakurda's outstretched arms. He wept over my head. Why? He knew nothing of my plight?

I thought he look a bit forlorn. Raji too was rather subdued.

Mataji had a long, private session with Thakurda. As we drove away, she gave me the gist of it. "I have told him that Dev is no longer welcome under our roof. He has violated our trust."

Quietly she went on, "Suman, I cannot protect you forever. Nor can you rely on Ved. I know he is my son. You yourself will have to tell off Dev. Can you? Will you?"

Was there a trace of pleading?

I took a deep breath, "I will." We headed straight for the capital's Ritz Hotel. Dev was summoned and received out of earshot of other tables on the lawn.

"Dev, have your posting orders arrived?"

"Why? They are not even due."

"I heard down south, Coimbatore maybe." He started.

"Coimbatore?"

"That should, I trust, put enough distance between us to bring you to your senses."

Dev turned on me. I met his gaze, my eyes boldly blank. "You have done enough damage. I almost paid for it with my life."

Mataji was icy. "Go to your own wife, Dev. She is a good woman. Let Suman bear her own husband's children. We will not expect to see you ever again. And, by the way, yesterday we were at Thakurda's...." the tone was ominous with portent. Turning her face away she got up and walked away, before Dev could whip up a suitable reply. I was at her heels. My gait was elegant enough, but my palms I found were clammy.

Thereafter, I refused to meet either Dev or Maya.

I had betrayed her willingly or unwillingly.

When Raji's daughter was born, I was pregnant. Mataji would not let me go. She wanted the baby to be born under her own roof, not at my father's home. At Thakurda's, no-one pressed the case. For all her love and care, I felt terribly hurt and cheated.

A year later, I went home. The house was beginning to look ramshackle; the annual coat of paint had faded. Thakurda looked distraught and Raji had lost her saucy confidence.

When I saw the face of my youngest 'sister', I knew why.

"Raji" I thought, "was willing game." There was nothing

more to fear from Dev anymore, but I never went home again. Not even for Thakurda's funeral.

Maya haunted me there.

Dada

As the years rolled by, Suman grew into a contented soul, but my heart bled for Maya.

She and Dev lived in a permanent boxing ring in their souls, tearing bits out of each other. Maya rarely spoke. Dev tried everything, from teasing to raving and ranting. No matter what he said, or how much he needled her, her response was a mute one. Not a word out of her. Only her eyes spoke and they flashed uncomfortably, demeaning him with their eloquent silences.

The only time he heard her voice was when there were visitors with whom too she spoke very little, but very effectively stripped him in public. Her tongue dripped acid very politely, as if questioning him for her every move and gesture, almost making him a laughing stock.

The boot was on the other foot now — sweet revenge for all those times that Dev had poked fun at her in front of guests. He dared not poke fun now for fear of it rebounding, and gradually rolled back the entertaining.

After all how long could he go on feeding people on old jokes when his wife refused to be the butt of any new ones?

Maya made long and regular visits home, restricted only

by the school schedules of her daughter, Lekha. Whenever she came, it took very few hours under Thakurda's roof to wipe out the tense lines which she brought from Dev's home.

But the transformation was deeper; it was easy to recognize the emptiness gnawing at her insides, washing away her limited beauty and turning her into a sharp-eyed shrew, constantly chewing paan.

The boys corresponded with me; they wrote that Raji hardly seemed to miss home; she had a large circle of friends and activities to keep her busy. It was the little one, Rati, who hungered for India. Every summer, there was a tantrum; and as she grew older, she would write to me, demanding to come to India. I trotted out weak excuses — droughts, floods, epidemics, riots, the house under repairs etc.

One year, Rati just turned up at my doorstep. I looked up from my book at the noise at the gate and saw two bedraggled souls seeking entry at the gate and then approaching me in the garden.

The girl was dressed in the loose shirt and skirt favoured by hippie tourists, her hair uncombed, except for a thin plait in the middle of her head, dressed in flowers. She pulled her companion, in long hair and dirty jeans to stand before me.

Taking off her dark glasses, she stood straight in front of me and gave me a long direct look. "Dada, I ran away to meet you. Don't you know me?" The voice was almost plaintive and the lovely eyes pleading.

I looked at her and felt my mouth falling open. I stood up; it hit me between the eyes. 'How could I have not recognized her?'

I placed my hands on her shoulders, looked at her carefully and then closed my eyes to contain the tears of thanksgiving. 'Thank you God.' Wordless thanks for the grace of the Almighty.

Slowly, I opened my eyes and allowed the swimming tears to wash over her head, as I pulled Rati into my arms. After a while, I again pushed her back and examined her carefully; How did I not recognize her? I examined every feature separately.

God had been kind to us. Time had done its work well. The early baby cast of her face, which replicated Dev's, had changed with the years. The eyes had taken on Raji's doe-like cast. Only the nose and lips belonged to Dev. The firm chin was not his. Except for those of us who knew, no-one would recognize her as Dev's daughter.

Thakurda's memory was safe. As I sent up another silent prayer of thanksgiving, Rati shrugged out of my grasp, crying plaintively, "Am I such a freak? What are you staring at? Meet Randy."

I smiled. "My little sister, who has grown into a beauty. Why are you in such rags? Doesn't your mother buy you clothes?"

"Dada! Don't be boring. We're hippies in India and

these clothes are fine, thank you," she pirouetted. "Mummy would want to stuff me into a sari, if she could. Please, we're hungry...."

I led them in and arranged breakfast, gazing at Rati and her boyfriend stuff themselves and lick their fingers. 'What had Raji taught the girl? I must take lots of photographs?' I thought to myself.

Two weeks later, Raji landed in India in response to my cable informing her of Rati's arrival.

I didn't recognize her too — grossly overweight, complete with a waddle and multiple chins. But the flash of the eyes and the charm of the smile were vintage Raji. She put out her hands in supplication, asking with that old smile of hers, "Must the past always haunt us?"

A part of me felt myself melting. Looking at her lush, polished appearance, I thought of the gaunt misery permanently etched on Maya's face.

'Has it been worth it?' I wondered. Justice would only be served when Dev and Maya arrived. Suman point-blank refused; had all these years.

Dev entered the house eagerly, a glint in his eye. He was stopped short by the sight of Raji at the foot of the staircase. He looked closely and perhaps in that instant, some fond memories evaporated. He turned away impassively: "Where is she?" leaving Maya face to face with Raji. Maya looked her stepmother up and down, noted the pain hidden at the back of her eyes. Raji put out her hands and repeated, "Must the past always haunt us?"

'Had she practiced that?' I wondered. Maya showed no signs of thawing. She turned wordlessly away. Lekha was bringing up the rear. Raji took her in, Maya's lanky frame with Suman's fragile beauty. For the first time some genuine emotion appeared on her face; regret flashed. Rati was less than a year younger than Lekha.

"Where is she?" Dev demanded.

I was off-hand. "Rati and Randy have gone for a walk."

"Who is Randy?"

"Randy," I announced with some relish, "is Rati's latest boy-friend, who helped her to run away to be a hippie in India."

The stunned look on Dev's face was worth the wait. Then his face took on a stern cast. "Where is she now?"

"Probably around; they should be home for breakfast."

"When did they go out? Did they not know we were coming?"

"They left for the Woodstock show two days ago and promised to be back today. Here they are now."

Ignoring Raji, Dev looked searchingly at Rati. She was her off-hand self, greeting him with a manly shake, "Howdy brother-in-law."

Dev was crestfallen. He raised an eyebrow at Raji, who shrugged her thick shoulders expressively. There was a cruel smile on Maya's sad face.

I was watching the whole play, which escaped the two young people totally. Dev was stunned by the appearance of Randy, by Rati, her clothes, her flippancy, so reminiscent of his own, once upon a time.

His expression said, 'Did I father this? What has Raji mothered?'

There was a pointed accusation in his eyes when he looked at Lekha, Maya's docile, seen-but-not-heard daughter.

I looked him full in the eyes and gave myself the satisfaction of remarking, "Can she erase her father's genes?"

Turning to look at Raji, I thanked God again for my bachelor status. One Dev and one Raji are enough for any family.

Dev quickly got over his initial distaste for Raji's gross appearance; she explained complicated health problems. Very quickly, their relationship slipped into the laughing camaraderie of twenty years ago; Raji's ready giggle was heard often, with their earthy humour and of course, nostalgia of Suman's wedding.

They moved out of their once-favourite corner of the central courtyard to the massive lawn outside. Raji sat on the swing, the awning shading her still delicate complexion. Dev sat on a cane chair, placed carefully just under the tree to receive the dappled shade.

Maya watched them from her bedroom window, as they

revived their short-lived past and caught up with the years in-between.

When she closed her eyes, Maya saw Thakurda's massive frame, taking in the silvery laughter on his beloved Raji's lips. She opened her eyes and blinked at the spare bald frame of her husband, leering flirtatiously at her stepmother, as he popped a tea-sodden biscuit into her open mouth.

From the vantage point of twenty years later, it no longer seemed to affect her. She even wondered why she had resented Dev's attentions to Suman or to Raji.

Try as she would, she could not invoke the old bitterness. She tried to pinpoint the emotion; it seemed more like relief. She was so close to freedom now, if she made the right moves. She crossed her fingers.

Taking advantage of the family's presence, Dev pushed his luck when everyone had gathered for breakfast.

"Why don't you invite your mother and Rati to come home with us for some time?"

Maya gave Dev her stone-faced look and raised an eyebrow in query.

"For twenty years, you have been making your point. Now let me have some time with my daughter," he bleated.

Maya gave him a mirthless smile and a knowing look. Dev could barely stand Rati and her Randy, eternally in tow. Even when Randy was not in tow, her modish flippancy jarred on Dev's old-fashioned paternalism; her questioning punctured his colossal ego. Dev's interest was obviously not in his daughter, but the daughter's mother.

Rati butted in unceremoniously: "Wrong number. I have only a few days left of my vacation and I want to see either Jaipur or that sex temple, not the back of beyond for one of Mom's old flames. I have plenty of old and new ones of my own to keep up with."

Maya took courage from the openness of the girl's approach. She looked straight at Dev, "I seem to remember that you often said that a mother had no place in a daughter's home. Go if you wish. I plan to stay here for some time. The festivals are coming and there is plenty to be done."

The others were stunned. Only Rati was unaffected. The tension at the table was palpable. My knuckles turned white on the spoon. Raji put her hand tight on Dev's forming fist.

"Twenty years ago," Maya continued, "I did not have the courage to say it. Now I can stand up and say, 'this is the man I do Not want.'" Dev started. "Do you have the courage to say 'that is the woman I want'?"

Maya drove home her point.

"Take her home if you want to. But do not ask me to be a convenient excuse. No one will even know about it. When they do discover, you will have settled in already. After some twittering, things will settle down, people will forget and you can get on with your lives. I intend to get on with my life here, at Thakurda's. Lekha's marriage can take place here instead of her father's house."

Dev drank from his glass of water and pushed back his chair to come and stand behind Maya. His tone was ominous. "We have private matters to discuss."

Maya's gait remained staid and measured as she went up the stairs with Dev's fingers digging into her elbow. Several pairs of eyes watched their progress.

"Any judge would give me an immediate divorce on the grounds of desertion."

Wordlessly, Maya marched deliberately to the cupboard, took out her purse and searched in it. She pulled out a pen and came to Dev, "Bring them."

"What?"

"The divorce papers. I'll sign them just now."

Dev retreated a few steps. "What are you talking about?"

"You mentioned the divorce. Did you think you were frightening me? Wake up Dev, this is not the 1950s when divorce was a living death for a woman, nor am I still 26 and scared of society any more. Oblige me, give me that divorce so I can come and spend the rest of my life in my own Thakurda's home. You retired after 25 years of service to the government to your ancestral home. I have put in as much time; I also want to retire to lead my life as I want to in my own home."

The fight visibly left him.

"Maya, what are you talking about? After all this time,

divorcing at this age; we'd be a laughing stock. For what?"

In the evening, the four elders congregated on the lawn. Rati was missing. Dev cocked his head at Raji, "Now you come to our house."

Raji gave him a considering look with a slight smile, "Dev, you are my son-in-law and I am your mother-in-law; Nothing can change that."

"Why not?" countered Dev carefully. "For twenty years, Maya has used you as a barrier between us. Now she wants to make a permanent break and come home, if not to Thakurda, then to her Dada. You at least come with me."

Raji's eyes swept over the foursome. She noted the sudden paleness creeping into Dada's cheeks and met a steady look from Maya. With a shock she realized that the emotion flooding Maya's face was relief.

'She actually wants out — a divorce?'

Raji gave Dev a speculative look and marshalled her arguments.

"What will people say?"

"Damn them," countered Dev. "We're too old to bother now."

Satisfied with what she had started, Maya got up and walked away.

"You still hold Rati against me, I know you do..."

"Of course I do and shall to the last of my days. What a mess you have made of her; and in all those years, you never.... This bitch would not give me your address. Now I'll have to take her in hand, more reason for you to come...."

"Fat chance you have of taking her in hand, as an old flame...." She giggled. "Nevertheless the offer seems interesting enough to be looked into; I still have a few more weeks in India before I go back and nothing particular to do..."

"What does that mean.... Am I a stop-gap gigolo?"

"No, a bald-headed one...."

Dada's chair crashed as he walked away.

The muted discussion continued into the night. Dada kept his vigil from the balcony. Well past the hour when anyone they knew would be about on the streets, Dada heard Dev's car doors open and then shut. The car moved towards the gate. No sound of footsteps entering the house.

White to the lips, Dada heard his own footsteps echoing silently as he went downstairs to lock the front door.

Bindi

"Oh no, you don't! Don't you touch him. You have no place here. That too, with that huge red bindi." The harsh words were bad enough. The look on his face was uglier. But the accompanying gesture, to pluck the bindi off her forehead, was too much.

Vandana caught Siddharth's wrist firmly and lowered it with a harsh stage whisper. "Don't you dare touch me? You have no business to talk about my bindi."

"You have no business to be here, you b****. You were not his wife. You only slept with him. Whore...."

Sharp looks and curiosity overtook the funereal atmosphere, as ears perked up for a 'family' eruption. The widow came forward to control her vitriolic son.

"Drop it Sid. This is not the time."

Her bindi was Vandana's weakness and her strength; her personal style statement.

All her life, her bindi had been important. The fondest of Vandana's earliest memories were of colourful bindis, the big one on her mother's forehead and the little red one on her own. Every day, she would painstakingly etch the tiny circle and then make sure it remained intact the whole day.

Her memories of her childhood marriage, at the age of four or five, were totally vague. The only memory that stood out was her graduation from a tiny dot to a larger bindi. But the memories of her battles for her bindi were sharp. She must have been barely six or seven when news came that the young groom had succumbed to the small pox. There was loud wailing and a pall of gloom in the house.

When Amma tried to wipe off her bindi, Vandana let out a loud wail that brought her Baba running. She ran to hide her face in his chest.

"*Meri bindi, meri bindi nahin lo...*" (Don't take my bindi).

They tried again the next day, to replace the red bindi with a black dot, but in vain. So they let her be. "She's too small to understand."

When the murmurs became louder, Vandana's father quietly opted for a job elsewhere, a reputed teaching institution which offered him a change of scene, a residence and scholarships for his children. Vandana and her brother Varun grew up on a leafy campus with lots of friends, a crowd with never too much money, but lots of ideas, all the encouragement in the world to do something, to be someone.

'Be not dumb driven cattle. Be a hero in the field,' her father often quoted to her. A deep anxiety would linger at the back of her mother's mind, but neither Vandana nor Varun ever really probed.

Then Vandana turned 18. She remembered the colours of her new outfit — green and yellow with touches of red, reflected in her bindi. Green and yellow bangles tinkled on her wrists, caught in a harsh grip by strangers, claiming to be uncles-in-law.

"How dare she wear these things? How did you allow her? We'll not stand for this. Enough is enough. You've had her all these years, now she must come home with us and live as she should, as a widow should."

Varun and Vandana were aghast. "Widow?"

Varun recovered and stepped forward, all of 20. Menace was loud in his voice and face. "If you ever repeat that word again, you'll lose your tongue forever. No-one here knows about it. If I ever hear it from anyone, I will know you have spoken. And then…?" His balled fists threatened silently.

"What will you do with Vandana? Who will marry her?"

"I will," a quiet voice spoke up behind him. Everyone

turned. Varun's best friend, Abhay, returned all the unspoken queries steadily. "I will marry Vandana and you need not trouble yourself on her account. This is between us and our families, not yours."

The uncles' mouths fell open in shock, then shut up. They cleared their throats. Before they spoke up, Vandana's father spoke quietly: "In the last so many years, we have never spoken about this. And we never shall. Your family has had nothing to do with my daughter in all these years. Let it remain that way."

Varun and Abhay collected the strangers' luggage. "We'll take you to the station."

"*Beta*, they are guests. Let them have lunch."

"Don't worry Ma. We'll give them lunch and stay with them till the train leaves."

Soon Abhay and Vandana became a pair. In fact it was a foursome, with Varun and Abhay's sister, Anita.

"We'll get married only after Anita. I'll tell my parents," Abhay said when Vandana's father spoke of meeting his parents.

To his parents, he just said, "I want to marry Vandana. We'll wait for Anita to get married. Meanwhile we'll both finish studies."

"Who is she?"

"Varun's sister."

"But who is he? What are they? We want to meet them,

to discuss...."

Seeing the protests rising on their lips, he held up his hands and said almost arrogantly, "Don't you have faith in yourselves?"

"Huh?"

"You taught me. Trained me to think. Trust in my judgment now. I'll marry Vandana only. Caste is all junk and you know what I feel about dowry. All the rest can wait until the time comes, after Anita is married."

After that his parents looked at Vandana in a new light as their future daughter-in-law.

She was ordinarily good looking, nothing spectacular.

The mould was classic, high cheek bones, large forehead, doe eyes; not very fair, yet well-mannered and educated by her scholarly parents. The high point was the smiling humour tucked at the back of her eyes. She smiled a lot, with her eyes and wisecracked intelligently, toning down the rather abrasive wisecracking of Abhay and Varun.

When the boys graduated from playground cricket to discos and cafes, so did Anita and Vandana. They went everywhere with the boys. In fact, were it not for the two brothers, both girls would have been labelled 'fast'.

And 'fast' they were. Secure in the escort of their brothers, they went everywhere, attended all the events and met everyone at all odd hours, way after all the other girls had gone home. They smiled easily, dressed glamorously, flirted outrageously and teased wickedly. College was more bunked than attended. After the novelty of bunking palled, all four took up part time jobs to pay for the glamourous lifestyles.

Soon college was over for the boys. Varun vacillated between law and IAS. And Abhay, the abrasive rebel, did a U turn and headed towards an MBA. In the last year of college, Anita was engaged to be married as soon as exams got over. When he came down for the wedding, Abhay had Vandana all to himself. But they had gone out together for so long, no one looked askance.

Except that the inevitable happened. Panic filtered through Vandana's voice.

"Abhay, I'm overdue."

"For what?"

"Abhay. My period has not come."

"So what? Talk sense, V."

"I ...I...I could be pregnant." Finally he understood. But he didn't panic. At the chemist, he asked for a pregnancy test kit and held Vandana's hand as she went through the motions.

"What'll we do now? Should we tell them to start the wedding preparations?"

"No. It's too early yet. I'm not ready."

"Abhay! Not ready yet after almost four years."

"I have to finish my MBA and earn a packet. Enough to lead our own life in our own way, not dependent for anything. We have to wait. Don't say anything to anyone," he said with a glint in his eye. "I'll work it out."

The next day he walked into her office, mid-morning.

"Make some excuse to get out and let's go." Outside, Abhay thrust a little box into Vandana's unsuspecting hands.

"Put this on" — a tiny *mangalsutra* set in diamonds twinkled at her.

"Oh Abhay so cute! You put it on for me."

"Don't be silly. It's artificial. Just to show the doctor. Put it on and cover up with your dupatta," he ordered curtly. They went right across town to a seedy suburb and within a couple of hours, Vandana was back at her desk. But less than an hour later, a colleague escorted a green-to-the-gills Vandana home to rest.

When her mother peeped in on her, Vandana turned her back, only to hear her exclaim "You've stained the bedspread." She sat up with an effort, grabbed the cover and took refuge in the bathroom.

Within less than a year, the episode repeated itself. Abhay was untouched, but Vandana could feel the physical changes in her body, especially her breasts, which she hid behind thick kurtas and dupattas at home.

But Abhay liked her in jeans and sexy knitted tops. On her next visit to his home, his grandmother's sharp tongue followed her eyes.

"Abhay, Vandana's becoming a woman, almost a

mother." She looked knowingly at them, eyeing the red bindi on her forehead and at the *mangalsutra* dangling at her throat. "When?"

"*Dadima,* don't talk rot," Abhay cut her off and hustled Vandana away. But she sensed a slight coolness creeping into their relationship. She often caught Abhay looking at her speculatively, when a big deal was coming his way.

"Join us for dinner and be nice to the guys. I want a big commission out of them," he would instruct.

The speculative looks came back when a friend got married with lots of goodies from the in-laws. Abhay was often pre-occupied, writing application letters to big firms. Once in a while, he was off for an interview and any visit to his home in his absence was pregnant with pauses, unspoken questions and speculative looks which made the otherwise chirpy Vandana distinctly edgy.

One day, the bomb dropped.

"I've got a job on an Assam tea-estate."

Was she expecting this?

"And....?"

"And what?"

"What about me? Do we ...."

"No," he cut her short. "We don't get married yet. I have to go and get settled in first. It's a strange new place...."

"We can do that together, you know."

"No." There was finality in his voice. It worried Vandana

and her parents when they heard it. The whole town talked and blamed Vandana.

"Easy lay. Now he's fed up." His letters and calls slackened. When Abhay came home after three months, there was distinct coolness, both in him and his parents.

Vandana heard stage whispers, "When will she get the message?"

She had never had anyone in mind until Abhay and no one else thereafter. Yes, when the boys would flirt outrageously with other girls right under her nose, she had remonstrated and he had been offhand, "It's only social time pass. It means nothing."

After that both Vandana and Anita had done similar 'social time pass', taking it very lightly; but that social time pass now came to haunt Vandana when rumours of Abhay getting hooked up with the only daughter of a big businessman began to do the rounds.

"She was of loose character in any case, running around all the time," was the popular vote, overlooking her other companions, Abhay, Anita and Varun.

Vandana wanted to get away, from the campus, the small town gossips, and the limited scope at work; but her parents would not let go.

"No, no Mumbai jobs. There are plenty right here," insisted her mother. But the firmness lost its edge when the rumours of the quick marriage of Abhay with the rich girl flew thick and fast.

"Vandana, why don't you take up that Mumbai offer? It is a good break and a much bigger post?" Vandana took up the Mumbai assignment for her advertising firm — to nurse her heartache away from prying eyes.

Mumbai, as a resident, not a visitor passing through, was a whole new experience for her. It was a vibrant city. Everyone was busy and so different. She felt free — free to be Vandana, not Abhay's girl, not Dadu's little sister, not Baba's daughter, not the hot chick in town — just Vandana. The new found freedom and confidence found reflection in her work and she was asked to stay on in Mumbai.

She grasped at the lifeline, quickly organizing her life as a PG, a veteran local commuter and a student of human nature on the locals. In a very short while, she was able to study her fellow passengers to draw keen insights into their personalities and philosophies of life. It was a game she excelled at.

> 'See that one, so carefully elegant, starched sari just so, pearl string, pearl earrings, one ring, and two bangles. She's been brought up right — which colours to wear when, subdued elegance, not a hair out of place. If she marries the right guy selected by her parents, she'll grow old quietly, elegantly, like... see that Aunty there, she's the wife of a retired big wig, maybe an Army officer. She hasn't gotten over her cantonment style of dressing. Everything has to match.
>
> 'There on that bench are her opposites. One's bindaas in her dressing, with loud prints and pants, and horribly

unfeminine but comfortable shoes and the other positively dressing down. That one couldn't care less how she looks. Why?

'There could be many reasons for that, all valid.

'She may be beyond marriageable age and not really bothered; actually she may be relieved that the hunt is over and there will not be too much pressure now; glad to get the family off her back finally. Now she dresses to please herself and her comfort, rather than how she would look to prospective in-laws.

'Or she may be genuinely bindaas, couldn't care less.

'Or it could be a form of rebellion from the constant pressure to conform, to look good. Why? For what? To attract a male? But she doesn't want to attract any male. Can't stand them? Is she dressing down purposely to spite her Man?

'Or has she left her husband or been widowed and now there is no pressure from her man to look good and not make him ashamed in front of others... so many reasons.

The *bindaas* babe, *buddhi ghodi lal lagaam*, is like that loud sari lady there. They have their husbands well under their thumbs. Few men want their women to stand out in the crowd. They want their women to look good. *Bas*. Other guys should envy but not pant after their women. But why should they give in to the whims of the guys? Why not some guys give in to the whims of the gals? If I want to dress garishly, I'll do so. Tomorrow I may want to be soft and sweet, I'll do that too. You mind your own business; shut your mouth and keep out of my way.

'Women must dress to please women and themselves. Why should they always dress to please some guy? It's okay if you are engaged or going steady and want to hang on to your guy. But all the time? Why? Do they please us all the time? Why should we? If I feel more comfortable in shorts, but my legs are not long and sexy, so what? Does that mean I should not wear shorts at all? Who said that only long and sexy legs should be in shorts, not plump ones, dark ones, or short ones?

'See that Aunty there? She is dressed to kill. But does that hide the wrinkles on her face, the look in her eyes? I think she looks better the day she dresses her age and smiles with her eyes?'

The comments were naughty but incisive. Vandana was growing up.

'Why is crying de rigueur at marriages? she asked. Hardly is the wedding over then everyone dissolves into tears. Not just the bride, but her entire family, sobbing away for all the world as if some major tragedy has befallen them.

Yes, there are many for whom marriage is nothing but an unmitigated disaster. Why then marry in the first place? But, the usual run-of-the-mill arranged or love match, is arranged well before-hand, much anticipated with flurries of shopping and rituals and glamour and giggling. Why then these tears?

'Are the tears not an insult to the groom and his family? That the entire bridal party is taking for granted that they are going to torture the bride, so the apprehensions over her leaving home, never mind the glamorous trappings. If it is a stranger and the bride is walking away with an unknown entity, some apprehension is warranted. But if the bride is getting married of her own free will, to a guy she loves?

The crying of the older women can be understood. They are weeping at one more falling into the marriage trap. Is marriage such an onerous trap? Who has made it so?

First social rules were formulated to throw the two together, for better or for worse. Looking at nature, it sounds totally unnatural, doesn't it? Then the males of the species, feeling threatened, created rules to maintain their foothold and inflicted those rules on society forcibly.

Why? Just so the male can have his way with her? And to give it a fancy touch — the rituals and ceremonies?"

Baraats are a constant travelling companion. Brides' fathers, often a garish lot, breathing down the necks of daughter, wife and other sundry ladies in the family.

Vandana had a field day.

It is Mothers who are supposed to be obsessed about their daughters' fates. That they will soon have to bear the woman's traditional burden of two families.

But just look at that guy and the way he is going overboard at the thought of a daughter getting married. WHY?

There is something very typical of men who go overboard over their daughters.

Suddenly, as the wedding approaches, their egos start hurting at the thought that Baby Doll will find someone more attractive than her Old Man.

And worse, they begin to view their own marriage in flashback. Every sadistic detail is recalled; those little games of emotional torture and blackmail they lashed their own wives with. Then they inwardly pale and cringe at the thought that someone is going to do the same to their beloved daughter.

Of course, they can never admit that to either wife or daughter. So bombast is the only solace. And since it is bombast, then why not overdo it?

Que sera, sera, what will be, will be.

"No more rose-tinted lenses. I don't trust anybody, especially if he says he wants to help me," she told friends. "He must have some motive, actual, imaginary, speculative or whatever. No one does something for nothing."

"Don't say that. You are breaking my heart," responded Kishore, the next door neighbour, enchanted by the chirpy new young woman on the block.

"Better your heart than mine," responded Vandana. But she could not hold off for very long the ebullient guy, who courted her assiduously, full throttle Punjabi style — loud blown kisses, jokes, dates, flowers, the works. Vandana held out for more than a year, until finally, the parents on both sides got together. Baba was blunt, Kishore expansive.

"What does all that matter? Did Vandana even know that guy? You can't punish her for what was essentially your mistake during her childhood."

The marriage was off to a heady start, after the simplest of ceremonies and a lavish spread for friends and colleagues. Could trouble be far behind? Friends and colleagues made social demands and Kishore was not always happy to be Vandana's appendage, more so when he was drunk.

"We always seem to be meeting your friends for dinner. When do we get to meet my friends? Or don't they count in our universe?"

Vandana was five months pregnant when things got out of hand. An evening of drunken roistering ended with a massive thrashing with Vandana black-eyed and bruised blue, protecting her slight belly.

"Don't you Kishore me. All evening you were talking to

other guys. Whose kid is that you are protecting from me? How many more have you had and not produced?" Vandana bit her lips, choking back the reply and the cries of pain. The old people were across the corridor, fast asleep.

She was examining the facial damage in the mirror when Kishore got up.

"You expect to go to the office like that?" Vandana covered her face up with her dupatta and goggles, leaving her room at the last possible moment to avoid questions outside. She headed away from the station and spent the day walking miles to nowhere, examining her soul for options?

'Where do I go? Home? No. What will the in-laws say? They idolize Kishore; will they believe that he has beaten me like this? For what?'

When she reached home, Kishore was waiting.

"You did not go to the station this morning. And you did not come from the station just now. I was watching. Which lover boy were you with all day?" Vandana swept off her disguise. The black eye had turned a violent purple and swollen; her face looked grotesque. She had not seen it, but could feel it.

"Who do you think can spend the day with this?"

Kishore let fly again. This time, Vandana fled the room. In a headlong rush, she braced her hands to avoiding slamming face first into the door frame. Kishore's kick caught her on the side. She crashed into the dining table and collapsed on the floor. The lifespring of their would-be grandchild oozed out before the awe-stricken eyes of her in-laws, surrounded by their bahu's broken bangles and her smashed-in face.

"I was told that you loved your wife to distraction, Kishore. Is this how?"

The tone was caustic. Mona Masi was known alternately for her bouts of generosity and her acid tongue. This time, Kishore was getting the full treatment of the latter. The old lady was on her annual visit to Mumbai and had taken a liking to Vandana. Now she laid down the law:

"This is no way to treat a daughter-in-law. Vandana needs to get away from here. I am taking her away with me. You decide what you want to do with your life."

"Beta, it is for the better. She needs rest — physical and emotional to get over this. And the distance will make both of you grow fonder. It always helps," added his mother.

Kishore shrugged his shoulders. He knew there was no arguing with Masi. More importantly, he knew that no excuse he offered would be valid as an excuse for what had happened. The baby gone, the office calling to find out why Vandana was not at work, the obvious signs of violence on her body and of liquor on his breath.

For perhaps the first time in her life, Vandana hesitated to put her bindi in place.

'Do I still have the right to it?' she wondered.

Kishore had not called in all these days. Three weeks in Mona Masi's lavish *haveli* had washed away all signs of Kishore's thrashing from her face. The daily massage by an experienced maid had polished her figure and skin to perfection. She was ripe for living once again as the sparring with, her cook and the maid began to pall.

There was excitement in the air. "*Bai, Saab log aane wale hain,"* (the men folk are coming).

The family, it seemed, was not enthusiastic about the unwanted guest. Reason dawned quickly enough.

"Who is in the guest room? I have brought guests with me. Where will they go?" the icy demand came from Mona *Masi's* elegant *bahu,* the lady with the pinched face, the silks, the pearls and diamonds. Mona Masi was quietly diplomatic.

"Shift Vandana into the guest house."

"But your son uses that for official and conference purposes."

"He has an office for that in town. If need be, he can use the downstairs rooms. Vandana will be upstairs in the guest house."

It was a cute little annexe to the south west of the main house, screened off from the house and lawns by a cane and rose trellis. The proportions of the annexe made it almost like a doll's house attached to the main house. *Guda-gudi ka khel* was how the daughter-in-law described the growing intimacy between Vandana and her husband, Dhanraj.

But it went much beyond that, to absorb their whole lives, Vandana's and Dhanraj's. Vandana turned her back on the world, living and operating out of the annexe, to copywrite all Dhanraj's ads from her retreat. Occasional holiday forays took them, not to fashionable Goa but distant Assam or Kottayam.

Actually this was another short spell in Vandana's life. It took less than four years for the spell to be cut short, first by the news of Dhanraj's illness, then his decision not to tell his family so he could spend the precious months left with Vandana, rather than a family exasperated over the loss of its social life on account of his illness.

"They will not be able to cope with cancelling parties, engaging doctors and nurses, special diets, even if it only means ordering a cook to make it...." Dhanraj declared ruefully.

"Death is so much more glamorous, you know — the spectacle of a twilight funeral, the sparkling whites from Manish Malhotra and the overflowing sympathy...."

Vandana said nothing; only cut back on all but the most essential assignments. No more holidays, no more trips — even the annexe was abandoned for a secluded apartment close to the Tata Hospital for easy access. Dharaj would not countenance staying there.

Vandana's worries somehow took on the hues of her bindi.

What now? She anticipated an ugly battle and then another new start, all over again....

Carina's Betrayal

"He specially asked me to bring you tonight," Ajay told her.

"How did he know I was in town?" asked Carina.

"Beautiful unattached ladies aren't a dime a dozen."

"Did he ring today or earlier? Was it specially planned for today?"

"What are you getting at? What's special about today, except that it's Saturday night, so everyone can sit up late?"

"Ajay, the first meeting after the break is tough. After that, things more or less fall into place." The casual words were contrary to the tension coming through in Carina's voice. They reached the large white house. Carina pulled her lace shawl close as she stepped out of the car.

Ajay held out his arms to the ladies — Nina a tall plump

rose and Carina, rounded and petite. They heard, rather felt the hush accompanying their progress into the house. Speculation brewed in many eyes flying to another lady in blue inside.

Momentarily, Carina's hand tightened on Ajay's arm before dropping it to walk tall on her own — slightly separated from her loyal chaperones. She approached the five ladies in the center. Raj was missing. The family resemblance of the four ladies was unmistakable. The fifth, the lady in blue had her back to Carina, but the back was familiar.

Carina recognized Beeji, Raj's sister, a tall lanky lady with salt-pepper hair with an odd twist to her mouth when she spoke, which gave her a very sharp look. Next to her was her daughter Naina, refinement stopping just short of elegance. Something was missing. The figure was perfect; the feet shod in elegant sandals. Large eyes hid behind old world spectacles. Perhaps it was the sad pinched face: the perfect give away of a woman without a man and only the nagging of a mother to take to her bed at night.

Next sat Uma. 'That must be the younger sister I never met. She looks older with her silver-grey hair, a vivid contrast to Beeji's salt and pepper, along with her pleasing grandmotherly appearance.' Her perfect proportions gave her an elegance belying her advanced years.

Carina was directly behind the other lady in blue, who turned in response to the gradual hush in the room. Even

Ajay and Nina stopped in their tracks.

Carina's heart skipped a beat. Her palms were sweating. 'So he couldn't really get away from me,' flashed through her mind. The sisters took stock of each other as others in the room took stock of them. The resemblance was more striking than the differences.

Carina had curves in all the right places. Pink pearls at her ears set off the dull sheen of her midnight blue silk. A single rose emblazoned at her bosom which now heaved tantalizingly, lifting the single pearl in a thin chain at her throat. Lightly streaked gray hair was held in a little chignon with a tiny rose.

Facing her was Juno, a big, svelte figure wrapped in midnight blue lace woven with metallic gold threads, huge diamond earrings framing an elegantly made up face and sophisticated hair-do. So similar and yet so different. For beneath the make-up, elegant clothes and jewellery, the two faces could have been identical!

"Hello", both spoke in the same breath.

"How are you?"

"I always wondered where I'd seen her before," Naina burst out. "Now I realize she resembles Carina. How did I ever overlook it?"

Carina turned to her; "Perhaps because we only met twice and no photos to remember me by. I'm flattered though that you remembered what I looked like."

"Do you two know each other?" persisted Naina loudly.

The room had already broken into hushed whispers. Loud and clear, Carina spoke out, "Didn't your Mama ever tell you? Miera is my elder sister."

"Elder?" gasped the younger silver-grey sister. "Elder?" The gasp reverberated through the room.

"I've lived adventurously enough to be prematurely grey."

Raj walked in expertly balancing a tray with five glasses with different shades of amber. "Here you are ladies...." He stopped mid-sentence to place the tray on the table before them. As he straightened up, he gave a signal. Music flooded the big room. Raj stepped close to Carina. "My dance, I think," and swept her into his arms and onto the floor. As if on cue, the lights dimmed.

'For the life of me,' thought Carina wryly, 'I'll never know whether that entry was not carefully stage managed. He wanted me to tell them myself what he's been unable to tell them all these years: That he divorced a sister to marry the older one. As emotionally gutless as ever,' was her last coherent thought as she gave herself over to the bitter-sweet experience of her very first dance.

"You look good enough to eat. I've got to have you before the evening is out."

"You've got five watchdogs, including your wife, plus all of Delhi watching you," she teased.

The pleasure was evident on her flushed face. Pulling her close to feel his manhood rising, Raj looked intently at the sensuous heave of her ivory breasts. "What are you thinking?"

"That finally, after all these years, I'm dancing with you."

He started visibly. "What d'you mean?"

"You never took me to a dance; when you wanted to shake a leg it was everyone but me." Her eyes opened speculatively, "How did you manage it today?"

"What?"

"Actually take me into your arms and onto the floor. Distance making the heart fonder?" Her eyes grew bigger and bolder as the magic of nostalgia wore off. "You couldn't have missed me very much with a look-alike in your life."

"Jealous?"

"Shouldn't I be flattered? Imitation is the best flattery? You can't get me out of your system."

"Have you? You were as excited as I was, a little while ago."

"Old habits don't change with legal slips of paper. Can one deny nature?"

Before Raj could counter that one, there was a tap on his shoulder. The music had stopped and then discreetly restarted when they remained engrossed.

"Can't monopolize the lady all evening," spoke a deep voice taking over from Raj and swept Carina off on a glorious turn, in which she stumbled.

"Sorry, I'm not very good on the floor."

"That I'm not accepting. You were good enough to eat just now. How often have you two danced with each other?"

"Today is my first time on the floor," she lifted her eyes to take in the reaction and see him. With so many NRIs and pseudos, one didn't always connect the nasal twang to foreigners alone.

Alex towered over her, she thought with a little secret smile, picturing herself describing him to her teenage daughter — 'tall, over six feet definitely, handsome though dark, must be some mixed blood — dark eyes with enough grey to give that distinguished look.'

"Like what you see?"

"Uh huh. Have we met?"

"More than met now," he said, pressing the length of her against him boldly, drawing a titter from the drones.

"Do you have eyes in the back of your head? Everyone, but everyone is watching us."

"Want out?" the smile was big, for external consumption of their audience, but the eyes that gazed down at her were dead serious.

'What does he know about this?' she wondered. Aloud she said, "Obviously. I'd love to make a grand exit."

Hand firm at her waist, he walked her off the floor. Ajay and Nina moved into vision, their looks anxious. Carina forced a smile big enough to cover her own apprehension. After all, he was a total stranger.

'Ajay, I'm going out for a while. I'll get back on my own."

Then, as Ajay sought to demur, she added, "I think

the party'll swing after I leave. Don't wait up for me Nina," Carina smiled over her shoulder proceeding towards the crone party while he shook hands with Ajay.

Meira stood there, staring frigidly at her. Carina said quiet good-byes. Raj was nowhere to be seen as she exited, conscious of the sharp glances.

"I don't even know your name?" Carina spoke into the darkness of the luxurious car.

"Isn't having a kindred soul enough? If it makes you feel any better, I'm Alexander Demetrios."

It was a long evening, driving in a velvet darkness, talking about everything but what they had just left. Later Carina picked at the meal before her, but drank deep draughts of wine.

Her responses suggested attention, but she was distraught, eyes shadowed.

"Have you been married?" the question slipped out, catching both unawares.

Gently Alex responded, "Let's talk about it with something that'll help."

He lit a thin cigarette, "I know you don't smoke, but occasionally this helps."

"What is there to smoking? Isn't it just another myth like love at first sight?"

Carina refused the cigarette.

"Will talking about my broken marriage help?"

"Then what will?" The look on her face was no longer

distraught or shadowed. She drew an almost desperate breath. "What will?"

"Accept my prescription?"

Her "yes" was wordless, almost mindless. Alex propelled Carina to the lift with a firm hand at her elbow, 'as if to stop me running away' she thought in a distraught aside. Carina was in a trance — nervous anxiety and tension plus the wine had frozen the desperate sorrow in her eyes as she stood aside, watching Alex leading her to his suite.

She stood uncertainly at the window, looking down the great height.

"Not thinking of jumping out, are you?" the tone was humorous. She turned. Coat and tie gone, he held out a glass and the thin smoke. "Not tobacco. It's your Indian stuff to relax you, I promise." The smile was reassuring. Carina placed it tentatively between her lips, wondering what she had gotten herself into.

"What the hell," she thought, inhaling the smoke. A great calm settled over her. Drawing Carina into his arms, Alex pressed his sensuous mouth on her frightened one, drawing out her soul. His hands splayed across her back, pressing her closer till he relinquished the lips, moving down her dimpled throat to the smooth ivory of her breasts.

Despite the novelty, he was able to remove her blouse with almost practised ease. At another time, it would have drawn a speculative gleam or a bracing question. But at this point, Carina was not quite lifeless, just another self looking down at her own self in wonder.

Gently Alex led her to bed, running a teasing finger down her spine. Then he drew her out, gently yet masterfully, evoking a strangely virginal response from deep within her till finally the storm subsided. Alex swept away the slow trickle that seeped out from under closed eyelids. "Tell, luv."

"It was wonderful."

"But it hasn't helped?"

"Do first times ever?"

"They make for great anniversary remembrances."

"My second."

"Second?"

"Today would have been our silver anniversary."

Alex sat up with a start. "Silver…! and blue Juno?"

"My elder sister. I saw them myself, right under my mother's nose."

"And?"

"I refused to face him — them. I would have lost the battle if I had. A lawyer friend cleaned up the mess; they had to leave town. This is my first visit to Delhi since."

"Shall we take our revenge on buddy boy?"

Carina turned around. Turning back, she took a deep breath to face Alex, a gleam in her eyes. "One condition. It'll not be revenge on him. I want to know how much more there's to sex than what I've had so far."

Divorce Medley

"What brings you home, *na taar, na itela, na din, na tyohaar*?" (no news, no special day or festival).

"Why? Is my home only open to me on festivals, not otherwise? Girls do come home after marriage, don't they? What are you doing here?" Preeti neatly turned the tables on her elder sister.

Suchitra responded self-consciously, "I've come on a visit for some time."

"So have I."

"Good," father played the peace-maker. "How's Shail, why didn't he come too?"

"Hardly likely. He's busy organizing the divorce...."

Ominous Silence. Preeti looked around, satisfied with the impact of her oh-so-casually spoken words. A single word broke the silence, "Why?"

Her father's face was uncompromisingly stern as he waited for Preeti's response. Her composure slipped slightly: "You don't expect your daughter to put up with a mistress?"

Father's tone remained clipped, "Your sister has."

The intonation flexed to a mute question, 'Why not you?'

Preeti's eyes questioned her silent sister shrinking in her chair. "What on earth are you doing here?"

Her brother answered. "Dhanraj is getting married again. Suchitra's here to give them time to settle in at home. She'll stay a while and then go back."

"And you, dear brother, will take her back to face that living Hell, just so...."

"So what?" the query was sharp.

Preeti took a deep breath. "You know what the trouble with us is? We're always so busy quarrelling with each other, we not only allow ourselves to be invaded and subjugated, we actually invite enemies to do that to us, while taking pride in our dirty blue blood. Look at you! Instead of asking how Dhanraj dare set Suchi aside, you're ready to send her back and are going blue in the face over my divorce. This, brother dear, is only the beginning. Shail thinks it is so simple organizing a divorce. But I'm not letting him get off scot-free just like that. I've told him in a very civilized fashion to meet my lawyer and the lawyer has been fully briefed on what demands are to be made."

"What demands are you making? Are you going to demean us with that divorce and then beg him for money to live on, as if your parents can't feed you?"

"You really want it both ways, don't you? In the first place, you don't want the divorce. Then you want it to leave me at your mercy. No, Sir! I want my freedom and my independence."

"Isn't divorce freedom enough?"

"Without a roof over my head and money in the bank? No."

"Now, you'll tell us that you have asked for a house as...."

"Of course, I'm entitled to an alimony or a settlement to maintain myself and my children in the style we are accustomed to. So either Shail has to repair his ancestral house and hand it over to me or vacate the new flat and go and live in that *haveli* and repair it at leisure. My children and I cannot live in that ramshackle place in its present condition. That's why the flat was bought in the first place, remember. The divorce cannot go through until and unless I have a house and money in the bank."

"Where will that come from? I've heard he's already heavily drawn from the market."

"Well... in that case, he'll just have to sell either some of his horses, or one of his companies, or some shares or a treasure or two from his ancestral home."

"Don't be a fool. Such things are never sold. Suppose he

sells some property that we gave him when you got married, or his share in one of our companies?"

"More fool you. Instead of putting them in my name, you put them in his name. Suffer now for the sins of the past."

"Do you realize that if he gives us a part of his companies, he may withhold the dividends on our shares, while we'll continue paying him on his shares in our companies?"

"Transfer those in my name; he'll not touch your tail then."

"I'll still lose my interest in his companies — forget it, Preeti."

"And let him off scot-free? Why should he get off scot-free? He's wrecked my life, my little world. Now I want to be free of him. I don't want him back. No sir, no thank you; I am happy as I am; but why should he get off scot-free? To do to another what he did to me? Look I'm not enjoying this. The thought of fending for myself and my kids is scaring the daylights out of me. Why do you think I came home for a breather? I sit up nights thinking — suppose the company goes broke, the shares drop, the interest stops or whatever, what'll become of me then? It is so much easier to succumb and leave all those hassles to others. But I won't; I can't accept his mistress under my roof. As long as he was going around with her outside, it was tolerated. But at home, under the same roof, in front of the children? No, no and again NO!"

"You mean he brought her home?"

"Yes, a shameless woman who said, 'I don't mind if they're around; how does that affect me, so long as we have our own rooms and lead our own lives.' She has her eyes on the *haveli*, maybe I'll also make a play for it; make him repair it first, that'll bankrupt him alright, then he'll forget all about the divorce and be stuck with this judicial separation."

"Where are the kids?"

"At home with Papa and his sweetheart. Let him learn to look after his kids. I'll insist they keep them half the holidays; after all I need a break too. And pay all their expenses, maybe even boarding school. If he wants a harem, he'll have to afford maintaining it. Let him learn to work hard, instead of living off my family. Do you want to support his mistress?"

Suchitra's story

"I was tired; bone tired with all the running around, travelling to way-out places. Your brother-in-law is crazy about the outdoors — trekking, camping, rivers, seas and what not. But I'm sick of it all. I never was the outdoors type in the first place. In all these years, I've learnt to barely tolerate it. Believe me, I've tried to get used to it: waking at ungodly hours, tramping for miles, the ghastly hunts, the flies, the insects, the raucous shouting, hooting and over-hearty laughter, hundreds of miles from civilization.

I tried all that for his sake. Even during my pregnancy and afterwards, lugging around a baby and nappies and what not. But God, now I'm tired of it all. I wanted some peace and rest so badly that I didn't quite realize that suddenly he had stopped insisting that Uma and I accompany him on every trip. He used to throw such tantrums if I refused to go earlier."

"When did that happen? He must have known that you didn't like the outdoors life?"

"I never quite realized when it happened. In any case, what did it matter to him what I wanted? That was how he wanted to lead his life. Lead — mine was but to follow. He wanted trekking and camping and hunting and fishing. I couldn't even remain a vegetarian.

"When we were in town, no question of relaxing, of a movie, a play or a *mushaira*, or anything cultural. It had to be a barbecue in the garden with the same hearty crowd, trading stories of treks, planning the next trip, reliving the last one. It used to jar on my nerves.

"If I even wore a sari, it invited comments. Remember all those lovely ones in my trousseau? I did not wear a single one. I spent my honeymoon in dungarees, fighting off mosquitoes with liberal splashes of Odomos, to the background caterwauling orchestra of dogs and cats."

"Then why not a divorce? Simple surgical cut, final...."

"No, no such hassle for me. Can you see my in-laws allowing it? What would I get out of it except the hassles?"

"What are you getting now?"

"A status, a position. I will always be Badi Begum (the elder wife). And I'll be free to stay home and live as I want, instead of trekking in the wilds or in the stock exchange like you."

"That is all very well for you two girls. What about me?"

"What about you, brother dear? What seems to be your problem — losing brothers-in-law?"

"Do you realize, Shail will take over our shares in his company and hand over his shares in our company to you. I lose out both ways."

"So keep his shares in our company — why did you put them in his name instead of mine at the time of the dowry giving? Wasn't that to have been my share in any case?"

Jai Ma

"Take this prasad for your husband. He just lies there, let him sweeten his mouth."

Reluctantly Anjali took the prasad and headed home.

'Am I the only one in this world untouched by this festivity?' thought Anjali as she headed towards her quarters across the courtyard of her home. She realized with some pleasure that she was not limping anymore and that the ever present body pain was a little less too.

'Should I not be thankful for that?'

Everyone was in a festive mood. It was Vijay Dashmi, the day Ma had vanquished the Asura. Across the village, in the Bangla para, women were gleefully smearing each other with sindoor and giggling about almost anything.

A huge effigy of Ravan was being given finishing touches

by the village craftsmen and gangs of enthusiastic youngsters. In the Marwari and Gujju *paras, fafda* and *jalebis* were being consumed by the kilo to replenish the energies spent on nine nights of riotous garba, swaying and whirling to the mesmerizing *dhols* and *garba* songs which had everyone entranced and itching to join in. Even in the police para, the Puja festivities were rising to a crescendo for the immersion of Kali Ma. Everyone was celebrating her visit as they sang out for her return the next year.

Anjali slowed as her memories took over.

Married at 16 from a poor home to the only policeman in a farmer's family, Anjali's dreams were shattered on the day after her frugal wedding. Ashok had showed up drunk at night, hurling abuses and shoes at her before crashing into bed. Her sisters-in-law were stoic.

"You'll get used to it after sometime. He feels entitled to drink because he is a policeman and gets his drinks free."

Anjali discovered that Ashok was barely literate. It was his brutal hands that had got him the police job. The family was happy that the good-for-nothing son who refused to work on the land was at least doing something. The police job gave him some clout.

He had also learnt police torture tactics. With her hands tied behind her and a gag in her mouth, no sound emerged from their quarters when he thrashed her thoroughly, two quilts ensuring that no marks were left to justify the agonizing pain she would always complain of. Anjali often wondered whether the family was really so obtuse that no one had deciphered her constant aches and pains over five years.

She eased herself down on the top step as she mused, 'Should I not be thankful to Ma for the strength she gave me the day she arrived last week?'

She had been all set to take her life by jumping off the cliff after Ashok's last bout of thrashing. By some miracle, he had pulled her back just in time. And by Ma's grace, she had stopped herself from falling at his feet. Instead, she grabbed his ankles and tipped him over the edge of the cliff.

Ashok's face showed shock chasing terror as he flailed his arms. Instead of grabbing her, he mouthed 'Why?'

He grabbed at a little branch, which snapped with his rapid descent. That little break saved his life. He did not die. The villagers had pulled him up.

But the fall had done its damage and turned the tables for Anjali.

Ashok was paralyzed from his waist down and he could not speak. He lay on his cot, totally dependent on what little time she could spare for him now that she had begun to work to make up for the loss of his income.

"If I wanted to, I could thrash you like you used to thrash me. But what is the use of thrashing a lump of flesh that cannot even feel the pain. Don't worry, I'll not thrash you. The Navjyoti people have told me that they will get us a special cot with a hole for you. I will place it in the side verandah so the room does not fill with your smells and the cleaning woman will come twice a day to empty the pail and give you a wash. Ma has willed it, hasn't she? Today I will celebrate Ma…" She emptied her little box of sindoor into her little *thali* and ran off to join the revellers.

Kunti's Daughter

The house my father built stood on a little rise. Behind it, the three silent sentinels — the tall palms rose into the sky. Surrounded by a large orchard, the house rose graciously from an arched facade to four large airy apartments upstairs.

Baba used to say to my mother, "one for each of the girls and one for us." She would chide him gently, "As if they're going to live with us all their lives. Won't they marry and have homes of their own?"

As it turned out, Amla, the beauty of the trio never married. She stayed home with Baba and Ma all their lives and forever thereafter, mistress of the big house and its estates. Later Varsha joined her, after she left her husband. I, Revati was the family disgrace, with a runaway match. What succour could I aspire for, from the house my Baba built? The two Mesdames ruled the roost there, busy leading their own lives and those of the numerous relatives around.

"Aren't sisters supposed to help each other in need?" Revati demanded.

The other two looked at each other and then at her.

"First sit down and relax. Tell us what the problem is."

They exchanged a worried look as they sat her down and pressed a glass of water in her hands. She seemed to have put on some weight — at last? —- and was short of breath, which they could not recall her ever being before.

Revati was several years their junior, quite out of their league actually. Married several years now, everyone had given up hope of seeing her children. Rohan was actually a 'great guy,' of the typical 'Hail fellow well met' mould, large and expansive and loud; perhaps too affectionate for the liking of his two older sisters-in-law, who viewed his cheerfulness with a jaundiced eye.

'It is too much, too synthetic,' said their looks, though they never actually articulated the thought.

It had been a love match, which ran the gamut of family opposition. Revati and Rohan stood firm and when he landed a job with a prestigious firm across the country, they eloped. Despite the childlessness, from all reports, Rohan looked after Revati well. The sisters never actually visited her; but family and friends who had, were a mine of information.

"He pampers her too much — does all the cooking for

guests too — a perfect gentleman, except for his colourful language. She runs the house as she pleases — hasn't taken any job, even though they have no kids. He doesn't let any of his relatives visit, in case they make fun of her about the kids." The question marks remained, reinforced a few months earlier.

Rohan was transferred back. Instead of taking the company flat in town, he opted for a villa outside town, preferring to commute daily and maintain a convenient distance from all family and old friends. Revati seemed shy and retiring; or maybe it seemed so in contrast to her husband's loud gregariousness. She rarely seemed to have anything to say for herself.

Now she was trying to speak, but could hardly do so. "I'm pregnant, but I can't be — shouldn't be – whatever! Only the company doctor knows. Now he's coming here..."

It was totally incomprehensible to the older sisters.

"Slow down, you're not making any sense. What can't you be or shouldn't be?"

"I'm pregnant, but I shouldn't be."

"Why not?" consternation and concern chasing through their voices.

"I can't and the doctor knows it, the company doctor. Now he's coming here…."

"What on earth are you talking about? Why can't you be pregnant?" Varsha the eldest took the lead, pointedly and patiently taking one step at a time.

Revati took a deep, deep breath, to calm herself.

"You know, it's been ten years. We'd been through all the tests...." Revati blanched as she recalled the tortured past, putting it into words with difficulty.

Revati

I had always wanted kids, if not a handful, at least one, my own child — "limb of my limb, fruit of my womb, my own child."

Rohan drowned himself in other people's kids; brought them home and dumped them on me. I abhorred it. I wanted my own to mother, not nanny others' kids. Every month, I waited with high expectations, but in vain. After a couple of years went by, I got worried. "Let's get some tests done", but Rohan was indifferent.

"Have patience," he would say and plan another party.

I became insistent and finally he agreed to take me. The doctor examined me after asking innumerable questions. He wanted to test both of us but Rohan was adamant. "Test her all she wants. I'm absolutely okay, hundred percent normal and healthy; get it up whenever I want. Nothing wrong here."

The wait for the results was interminably agonizing. Finally it was time to see the doctor. "You go and get the result," said Rohan casually.

"I'm scared. Suppose it says I can't have a baby ever? What'll I do?"

"We'll cross that bridge when we come to it. Why jump the gun? Go and get the results first."

"I'm scared," I was almost in tears, "besides the doctor had said that both of us should go together for the results."

"You go, I'm busy this evening."

"Then we'll go tomorrow," I offered.

"For God's sake, why don't you go and be done with it?" He was getting irritable.

"Can't you see I'm scared? How can I go alone?" By then I was crying and shaking all over. That shook him and very reluctantly he agreed to take me, but the mood was abrasive. More so when the doctor announced that I had tested positive; there was absolutely no reason why I could not conceive.

He was furious. "What the hell do you mean by that? That I am a nincompoop? All you doctors are the same bloody fools — no practical knowledge, only book knowledge, damned fools..." The storm took its time subsiding. I admired the doctor's patient sympathy and reasoning; he did ultimately manage to get a sample out of him, only Rohan never went back to get the results.

Ultimately, I went — alone. Screwed up my courage to go and face the verdict — an abysmal sperm count, but never screwed up that extra courage to tell Rohan about it. The

matter was dropped and never mentioned. The yearning for a child of my own was submerged, until it surfaced years later.

"So what happened? How did you know that you are pregnant?"

"The urine test confirmed it. Rohan is so thrilled, I don't know what to do."

"What do you have to do, for Heaven's sake? Be happy with him for God's sweet grace after all these years. What are you wailing about?"

"Why don't you understand? At our farewell party, the doctor had seen me and told me to go in for a check-up; but with all that packing, I didn't do it. There was so much to do. Now he's coming here for some company seminar. He rang Rohan at the office yesterday and said he'd stay with us; he'll see me so obviously pregnant. Oh! what will I do?" she wailed.

The two older sisters looked at each other, still unable to fathom why the doctor's visit should call for such a dirge.

"Oh! for Heaven's sake, does one have to spell it out? It is not Rohan's baby. It is mine. The doctor knows that Rohan cannot possibly be the father?"

The accusations came thick and fast and tough.

"You were unfaithful to a husband who had implicit faith in you." The hectoring tone, so reminiscent of a far-off childhood served its purpose: it put her back up and the old steel spine shot up, making her think, hard and fast.

"I was unfaithful. Period. Don't go beyond that. If it is alright for a man to have another woman, why can't a woman have another man? Wasn't Kunti's first born otherwise? Why carry on and on about this *Pati Parmeshwar* rot? If you don't produce children with clockwork precision, they would have no qualms about hiring another womb in which to implant their seed. That is acceptable to you. So is hiring another man for the wife, if the husband is not effective enough. That is what they have been doing since time immemorial, part of our venerable cultural heritage.

"How did Kunti produce the Pandavas, despite an impotent husband? How were her husband Pandu and his brother Dhritarashtra conceived? It was not a case of hiring surrogate wombs, but surrogate penises to do the needful for their wives, who would then return to become 'chaste wives and mothers.'

"I have also done that — only in my case my husband did not hire the penis for me. I did it for myself! What's so abominable about that, which is not abominable about hiring a womb or a penis for one's wife?"

Revati bolstered up her case. Rohan was always on his own ego trip, considering himself the ultimate in husbands. "How can any woman ask for more?" Telling everyone how big-hearted he was to have kept me and not have married someone else.

"What would have happened to you, if he had?"

demanded Varsha. "You'd have been on the streets, you silly. My husband was a drunken lecher; he brought his women home. When the kids grew up enough to realize what was going on, he bought a love nest and took them there; I know, I used to have to send over food. I never fell into the trap you have. What have you gone and done?"

"It was really very simple. I was sick of myself; instead of raising a family, I was constantly entertaining, cooking and smiling for his friends. He didn't want kids; in any case, he used to say they were too messy. He was happy enough play-acting for everybody's benefit. Then someone quiet and self-assured and sympathetic came into our lives. He was a new neighbour. But he spent all his evenings with us. Come rain or sunshine, Lalit was there. We talked a lot. I finally got a chance to hear my own voice, instead of only Rohan's all the time. Was that such a crime?"

"What?" asked Varsha uncomprehendingly.

"Wanting to hear my own voice for a change? Wanting some respite from being made to feel grateful for remaining married? Wanting some gentle love making, verbal if not physical, for a change?" asked Revati.

"What changes are you talking about? Women are supposed to make changes to suit their husbands' choices and lifestyles, not dictate changes. See me, your brother-in-law loved to f..k and I hated it. I had to pretend and of course he guessed it and finally returned to his old girlfriends. He had them by the dozen. When his parents protested, to spite them, he started bringing them home. Yes, right there in our bedroom, in our bed. I didn't protest or find another guy. I just kept quiet," explained Varsha.

"How did you get the divorce then?" demanded Revati.

"That is another story altogether."

Varsha

Varsha took a deep breath. "Amla came to visit and your brother-in-law was smitten instantly. She was just his type, all that I was not — tall, fair, voluptuous, flirtatious and sexy,with a bottom that positively wiggled in invitation. Could a guy like him resist that temptation? Obviously not! He began to stay home. I tried to close my eyes as usual, but one day, the door was open and I walked in on them and was dragged in.

He banged the door shut and threw me on the bed. "Open your legs," he barked out harshly. Too scared to do anything else, I obeyed and he pushed my sister Amla's face between them." Steeped in old memories, Varsha recalled how after the initial cringing and shock subsided, she opened up to the new experience. It showed on her face.

"Now I've got you, you little bitch," exulted her husband, "now I know how to fix you."

Despite years of attempts to kill her spirit, Varsha still had some steel left in her. Before that new pleasure could suck her into a sorry vortex, she packed Amla off. He continued to bring his other women, sophisticated madams and glitzy professionals; only now the evenings ended with her shamed ecstasy. Varsha was well on her way to becoming a lesbian.

"At first, I hated myself and tried not to enjoy it. That was impossible. I didn't know what to do. You know, all my in-laws admired me for my fortitude in putting up with his nonsense. They always came in full force to show solidarity with me against him. The question was: How to crack up that image? The children were so young. What would have happened to them?

"One day everything came together. His mother and one of his lady friends landed up together. I worked at keeping the kids and my mother-in-law occupied outside in the garden, knowing fully well what was going on inside the house, but he kept shouting for me. Ultimately his mother insisted, "Go and see what he wants". I knew exactly what to expect inside. What I didn't know was what was to follow...

"In hindsight, I presume my mother-in-law must have knocked, but none of us heard it. Suddenly the door opened and as she grasped the scene she fainted. I was staring into the ashen face and traumatized eyes of my son Ashish. He took one sweeping look — the déshabillé, the guilt and the shame evident on the faces. He turned and walked out of the house.

"Five years now, not a peep from him. Where is he? What

is he doing? What did he see? What did he understand? How did he judge? I try not to think about him because whenever I do, so many questions rattle through my brain and drain it out. Amla is so good for me. She makes sure that I don't think about it."

"Stop that rubbish! You were enjoying yourself. All the while you were cursing your husband for forcing you into lesbianism, you were actually enjoying yourself," shrieked Revati.

"If the rape is inevitable, lie back and enjoy it — he used to say that. After all, he was my Lord and Master. I had to obey him," Varsha enunciated unctuously. "Why not smile and obey and enjoy, instead of weeping?"

"If he had asked a man to take you instead of another woman, then would you have allowed a man other than your precious husband? Would you have continued to smile then?"

The older sister looked distraught. She didn't answer, though her eyes said that she had given that question a great deal of thought.

"How did the divorce happen then?" Revati persisted.

"Amla. Amla came to town again and he proposed she live with us. Amla refused and he threatened divorce.

"Do what you damn please, it's your life and your wife." said Amla.

He wanted a divorce and I had nothing left there. After Ashish, the other children found hostels for themselves and refused to even visit home. All they said was that they did not want to put up with a drunken dad and a frozen mother. That both of us should live our individual lives in peace."

"So you left?"

"Around that time, Baba fell ill. I came rushing home, but it was too late. Amla was left all alone. She never married so no family, so I stayed put to keep her company."

"It was so convenient, wasn't it? Between you two, you divided up all Baba's possessions, since I was the family outcast. And then there was Amla. After all wasn't that why you came back in the first place?"

Varsha turned up a startled face, guilt writ large on it.

"How long are you going to be? Amla is waiting for you. She'll catch a cold waiting in this chill."

Revati gasped in surprise. This rasping tone of Buaji was one that she had never heard before. A tiny, fragile woman, dominated by huge eyes set in a small, mousy face, she had been a soothing background to childhood — always seen, always felt in warm hugs and smiles, rarely heard, except for prayers and blessings. This sharp tone, those flaring nostrils, that glint in the eye, was it excitement or madness? Revati's head reeled — is this *Buaji??*

Bony hands joined in prayer, clad in faded housecoats, inevitably of nondescript print. Even when she wore the occasional sari, the print remained nondescript, as if any definite print or color would have drawn attention to her when she only wanted to melt into the background; so soft that Revati often felt that *Buaji* would crumble if hugged too tight.

Revati could scarcely believe her eyes and ears: how much had that gentle demeanor disguised? Could childhood be so innocently blind? This was a woman scarce recognized, aged beyond belief, yet that glint in her eyes!

"Come, young lady, you're no longer a stranger to the pull of the flesh. Did you really think that your sister came here merely to do *seva*?" The old lady's eyes glinted; was it malice?

"Of course, she did do *seva* and she got the reward for it. Her share of the property, but more than that, she got what she needed most with the exit of her husband and the women he used to bring home; she got a fulcrum around which to rebuild her life. They do each other a favour. Varsha needs a fulcrum and Amla loves to be the fulcrum."

"And you?" asked Revati.

"I take pleasure in their pleasure. I have my Ramayan and Amla to fall back on. What about you? Why did you?"

"Don't give me that crap. All of you are sick. *Kirtans* and Ramayan and Amla. Have you ever read your books? Actually read them for yourselves and not what some fraud godman has to say? They talk of fidelity but willingly condone male infidelity, not female; except of course for procreation of heirs. Whose heirs are those?

"For years, I lived under self-imposed controls. First I wanted to live up to Rohan's expectations, always trying to act mature wondering, 'what will he think?' When I finally got over that, I was trying not to hurt him. Always thinking 'can't hurt him. This will make him feel older, that will make him feel bad, feel small etc.'

"All at once, I had a companion with whom I need not be careful of my words, my tone, my expressions, my feelings; with whom I could crack a joke without wondering if it would be taken in the correct spirit. It was such a relief, even more so because he was accepted in my household. He was not just my friend. He was our friend. It allowed me to relax. Was that so wrong? So evil?"

As Revati strode determinedly away, she realized that the visit home had enabled her to put together her thoughts, instead of wildly picking at a mass of tangled thoughts and not knowing what to do with them.

She knew that she would have to tackle the doctor on her own. Her sisters had helped — to put back the backbone into her life — her own life.

Law's Asses

Governments make laws and laws make asses of men who just put them away and do what they want to do. Who implements them?

Women have to fight to get what every law gives them — just the words are spoken; but the benefits need battles to be won. And so often, the asses use other women to defeat the women who should benefit. When will women learn – not to join the asses?

What made this battle particularly poignant was that Pinky was battling her own mother; yes, she who had taught her all she knew, she who had set her to work long before she should have, she who had made her work to earn money for her brother's education so he could land a good job.

Now the mother had succumbed to that age old curse:

'love for the son.' False hopes of a secure old age with the son who had, to date, lived off the fat of the land and the labour of his parents and sisters?

"Listen to me Pinky. He is my son, your brother, not any stranger. After all when all you girls are married and gone he will look after me. You girls cannot carry forward your father's name. Only he can. So I have to stand with him. Why can't you understand that? It is so simple. He is his father's son. That is why he got his job when your father retired, did he not? Even the government accepts that. Why can't you?"

But Pinky would not accept these arguments. She felt betrayed by the mother for whom she had slogged all her life, to support her in the never-ending battle to educate her children, run the home and earn enough for a roof over their head.

Today that roof was at stake!

A Sahib was roped in to mediate.

Pravin, a clerk in a government office was fuming at his mother's involving one of his office sahibs.

He said, "I am a graduate, working in the department since my father retired. For months I have given money to Ma to help her, although my wife and I did not live at home. How does that wipe out my right to the family home? One by one the girls will marry and go to their homes and Ma will be left alone. Then what will become of her? Better to sell the house and let her come and live with us, is it not?"

The mother took up the refrain. "Sir, it does not behove girls to interfere so much in their parental affairs, does it? *Kya zamana aa gaya hai, ladki hissa chheenna chahti hai bhai se* (How things have changed that girls today want to grab shares from their brother.) Sir! the truth is that girls have become greedy. Lord knows we spend money to educate them and all these new fangled notions are because of that? This girl did not study much, but she has absorbed plenty — especially that girls are now equal to boys in everything. She actually says that sisters and brothers have equal stake in all property, even a home. Can you believe that? Her father's ashes are not cold yet and she is inciting all her sisters; but can I forget? I know that Pravin paid for the house, so it is his and so is the bike."

The fury on the face of the accused daughter was pulsating as she turned accusing eyes on her mother and then turned to the mediator:

"Listen Sir. I will tell you the plain truth. It cannot be Pravin's house or Pravin's bike because he did not pay for them by himself. He has only contributed — that too a little bit. You want the full account? I'll give it to you. I am the eldest in this family."

"So what if she is eldest? Ask her did she not go to school? Did I not pay her fees?"

"Pravin is two years younger than me but we started

going to school together. And within four years I was taken out of school so that he could be given new school books and uniforms every year. My mother started working in houses while I looked after the younger children and did all the housework. She used to come home tired and Baba's pay was never enough.

"Then I learnt to do stitching and embroidery. With the money I earned, I paid for the younger girls' schooling but as soon as they could hold a needle properly, mother made them learn the work so they could help me earn more money, along with their studies.

"For what? You must know for what we needed the extra money. Extra money was needed to pay for tuitions for Pravin, first to pass Matric, then Higher Secondary and then go to college. To pay for special treats when he brought his friends home, went for movies and needed fancy clothes. For all that, all of us girls slogged.

"Finally, he became BCom pass. But Baba retired and his pay was reduced to a pension. His job went to Pravin. At that time, he started with a pay of Rs 800 a month."

"Sir," butted in the mother, "when he started to work, I used to give him only 200 rupees as pocket money and saved the rest for more than three years so that we could collect money for the down payment for this house. That down payment was from Pravin's money. So is it not his house?"

"I will give that account also. We girls slogged to get him

educated and to get that job. His initial pay went for the down payment, but what about the rest of the instalments? When all of us had to work, do cooking and embroidery to run the house, despite Baba's pay, how could it run on Baba's pension? All of us had to work — mother, Kinjal, Soni, I and even Chhoti. As soon as we bought this house, mother got Pravin married, thinking there would be one more pair of hands to work.

"But our sister-in-law is a real Madam who did not want to soil her pretty hands with embroidery or even cooking. Pravin also did not want her to work. In three months, he shifted out of the house to a new quarter, a house of their own. Besides, she told him that since he was educated and worked in a government office and would get a raise very year, she was entitled to her own home.

"So we started all over again, managing on the pension to run the kitchen while we all slaved to collect money for the instalments, college fees for the girls and their dowries: six mouths to feed, six bodies to clothe, three sets of books, notebooks, bus passes, plus medicines. I never bought a bindi for myself until I got married.

"Kinjal was pretty and so was Soni. They got married. Then I got lucky. Yes Sir, it was pure luck — my man did not see my looks, he saw my earning capacity and he was ambitious to go up in life; so he offered for me without any dowry; he even bought the wedding sari and the *mangalsutra.*

"I used my share of the dowry to clear off the remaining instalments of the house; so all they lost was what I used to earn from cooking and embroidery. But then, as if the need to pay off the instalments had taken the life out of her, *Mai* (mother) fell ill."

(Unconsciously, the angrily contemptuous mother gave way to a softer Mai).

"We became anxious again. Only Chhoti was left to look after her, giving tuitions to neighbourhood children to help the kitty. Finally someone shamed this *joru ka gulam* (wife-slave) and he started giving 200 rupees a month — for the last year and a half now. Against those two-three thousand rupees (the first time he has contributed for the household) he wants to swallow up the whole house?

"Has Mai gone soft in the head in her old age? How did it become his house? We fed him, clothed him, educated him from childhood to the day he left the house with his wife. Against all that, he has paid the first 20,000 and now 3000 — total 23,000 rupees for the 25 years he lived under my Baba's roof. That is less than a thousand a year, to take away the roof over Mai's and Chhoti's heads?

"They can't think straight; I can and I'll not give it to him. I have paid all the instalments from my earnings — bank cheques, and the total is much more than his 20,000."

Again the brother Pravin spoke, bursting out, "Sahib, she speaks nonsense. Married daughters have no right to the father's house after marriage. Doesn't the Law say so?"

"Everyone knows the Law is an ass — and so are you," declared Pinky firmly.

Losses

"Now see for yourself what she had, that you didn't, that made me ditch you for her."

"You really think I still regret that? I often wonder now at myself — what a fool I was! I spent ten years loving you and another ten regretting you, when I should have been celebrating your exit from my life. I was free at last, to get on with my own life, without any chains around my feet, no faithless lover to weep over, no husband to pamper, no rebellious kids to hold back from drugs and pre-marital sex. Look at what you've done to her," Monica pointed to Dimple.

"She had talent; you submerged it, just as you wrecked my career. 'Monica, don't work, you don't need to; I am there' you would wheedle. What happened to you? — chasing pieces of ass?

"Then she appealed to you, so you wept: 'Monica doesn't appreciate me, she tries to boss over me.' Poor kid; she was too raw to understand that you were laying the grounds for infidelity; she would never have dared to question you till it was too late to save her marriage; by then she'd outgrown you and your insecurities which demand the submergence of your mates."

Dimple spoke up. "Don't you feel lonely?"

"Do you?" Monica countered with a laugh. "You've been having your affairs since you left him. Now you've become discreet, because your kids have grown up. They need him. He needs you, so you strike bargains with each other, using the kids as bargain chips. Sooner or later, they'll refuse to be bargaining chips. I have no such chips, no marriage certificate and no kids. So, I fell on my own feet and learnt to manage my own life, making the most of the limited talents God gave me and the few friends who were not carried away by his charisma and his power to harm them."

"But the loneliness?" Dimple persisted.

Monica linked her arm with Dimple.

"Let's talk. Why are you so hung up on loneliness? Haven't you worked it out yet? Men have been brainwashing women with things over the centuries to hold them captives and bash them up. It's like all your womanhood is neither in your heart, nor your mind nor your soul, but only between your legs; that makes rape the biggest club to hit a woman with!

"So also loneliness. Suppose he had died, wouldn't life have carried on? If the kids had died? You would have learnt to fill your life with others. Men come and they go, don't make them permanent fixtures. Tell me, haven't you ever felt that he had messed up the kids for you? Didn't your Dad do it to you? If it weren't for your Mom, you'd be a wreck today — me too. So I satisfy myself being surrogate Mom to plenty of other kids. To tell you the truth I don't mind it at all. Not for me that messy mewing and puking; just nuzzle them happily, and then hand them back to Mommy dear.

"Don't let some male tell you I'm an unnatural woman. That is another myth they just love to propagate: that a 'woman is born to mother'."

I add my caveat: "Not all women. Plenty like me around, who were not born to mother; only they dare not admit it, just give me sly admiring smiles saying, 'atta girl, you said it'."

"You've missed the point," said Dimple. "You may hate men, I don't."

"Who said I hate men? Let me tell you I get horny too, so do you, so do others. It's human to get horny, but I like the men better grovelling before me, not the other way around. Maybe I had too much of that earlier, so the order reverses. It is Nature's law of change and I have changed. When I need someone, so okay, what's the big deal? Actually I'm getting old for that too now; it becomes more trouble than it's worth, isn't it?"

"He smothered me," Dimple burst out. "It was terrible. I was so naive and adoring. I couldn't speak up, and so I got smothered. Not allowed to speak, to express an opinion of my own, only second his; otherwise it was public denouncement as a nitwit in front of his uncouth friends. I often wondered how you could have trained him that way; I mean to behave that way with his women."

Monica snorted, "Why do you think he left me for you? I fought him every inch of the way. Initially his ego was so fragile, every failure was a mountain and I had to help him up; so I listened but later I started speaking up and pointing out things. It made him mad. Real mad because he hadn't seen these things for himself.

"That hurt his ego: that I saw, noticed and understood before he did. I pointed out to him, rather than the other way round. That was my death warrant; now I look at it as a release warrant, release from a juvenile's jail."

Dimple railed, "You got out, but I was in and after the initial glow, it was terrible: dull and boring and stupid. I didn't want to do the things he did, meet the people he liked; it was so dead, so stultifying. He admired bold women, but His Woman had to be shut up at home out of sight, bearing kids. That was our end. He was thrilled to be a father, but not of girls. The day he first cursed me for producing two daughters in a row and hit me when I said it was his genes, I decided that I would leave him. But I would not just go;

I had to hit and hit where it hurt."

"What did you do?"

"I had barely come home after the baby when he was on top of me. 'I want a son', he said. And I decided that he would never have that son. I allowed myself to get pregnant, taking all the possible steps for a son — the douches, lunar dates, special diet, the works, everything. I got pregnant and when the sonography showed a boy, I took the girls away; Never told him till later. It would have been no use — he'd have found a way to stop me and I knew I couldn't fight him. Can one fight a hero? No!"

"So, I just went away, parked the girls with my mother, left town and had an abortion."

Monica gasped. "But it was your baby as well...."

"But with his genes which he would crow about. No thank you! I knew I'd have my hands full raising these two on my own. No more, I had it sealed off — the end."

"Does he know?"

"Of course, much later. Why d'you think I let the divorce simmer for so long; let the penny drop. Not that it had its effect till much later in life, much later, after his girlfriends got married and went; he was alone and no longer successful, this time without an unlucky wife on whom to shift the blame. Much later, he started accepting what a pig he was; but by then it was too late. He had missed the girls' childhood. And when he came to me, I told him about the son...."

Lila Aur Marathan

"Do you want him to remain a yokel forever tied to the plough? There's lots of money to be made in a city. You'll live like a queen when he takes up the city job," Ramu was persuasive as he addressed his daughter Nimi.

She caught his eye and glanced around the dilapidated courtyard with its open kitchen and animal shed, and her dishevelled mother slaving over the smoking *chulha*.

Her eyes asked him: 'Is this how a queen lives?'

Aloud she declared firmly, "I will not marry any city boy, even if he belongs to this village." Nimi looked delicate but her voice was rock steady.

Even more exasperating: his parents sided with the stubborn refusal of Nimi and his own wife Lila that if Dilip went to Nasik, Nimi should not marry him.

Baoji spoke up. "Beta, things are changing here. Now they ride tractors to the market. They rent DVDs to see films at home and eat pizzas with Coke too. If Dilip wants to go with you, take him."

Ramu stomped out. He did not stay long. Instead of his usual month's stay, he left within ten days, leaving behind a household sighing with relief at the exit of tension. Before he left, there was another dust-up. Ramu wanted to take with him not just his friend's son Dilip but also his own son Raghu.

When he announced his intention, it was not just Lila who paled. The old people were left almost gasping for air.

"Beta, don't you realize Lila is getting old too? Who will help her with the farming if Raghu goes with you? Hasn't she slogged enough for us? She came as a young bride to help your mother and has looked after us and the land ever since. She was younger than Nimi when she came. When you left, she took on all your duties along with your mother's. This has been a female headed household ever since. Now newspapers write articles about them. What did the government do for us? What have you? Have you any idea of what she has been through all these lonely years? You want to snatch her only hope for the future?"

Stunned by the old man's forcefulness, Ramu took a while to point to his son:

"Look at him; my son is eager for a city life. You only want a slave; his father wants to give him a chance to become a man. Don't I need someone of my own with me there?"

Lila glanced at her son. He flushed at the scrutiny but the excitement was patent. Her heart thumped loudly and her womb seemed to shrivel with pain. 'How can we hold him back if he wants to leave us and go? Should we?'

Apprehension broke out as sweat on her face. She had been on her haunches, churning butter in the traditional way, twirling the long stick-churner set in a big pot. Now she sat down heavily, thinking:

'The roads of Nasik are not paved with gold. Ramu had promised me that, but never sent enough for two square meals. That came off the land if I worked hard enough. During the monsoon, when we needed cash most for food, seeds, fertilizers, everything, it was always his lean season too,' she recalled.

Money was not the issue here. The issue was losing Raghu to the city.

Nimi was watching her mother. Once, only once had Lila gone to visit Ramu in his city. Bebe had told her that in the context of the dramatic changes seen in Lila after she came back from the visit. Yet nine months later, Nimi had been born.

Ramu took another tack. "Let me speak to Nimi."

His father responded in a conciliatory tone, "She's your daughter so who can stop you? Nimi child, listen to what your father says."

Ramu shook his head. "I'll speak to her alone." As he took Nimi's arm to lead her out, apprehension clouded three faces. Raghu was oblivious. They left home, heading for a little glade by the canal. Ramu started off, he thought gently. "Nimi, I am not your enemy but your father and you are my daughter. I want the best for you."

Nimi's eyes remained downcast, but her face was skeptical.

"Look child, I grew up here, in this village and have now spent years in Nasik. I know the difference believe me. Life is totally different there. Things are so open, so free there. With Raghu and Dilip, we'll soon be earning enough for you to come there and you'll have the latest fashions to wear and the latest films to see in big theatres."

Ramu faltered at the scorn on his young daughter's face. "How can Dilip afford a wife in Nasik when you have not been able to afford your family in over twenty years?"

"If Lila came, who would have worked the land and looked after Baoji and Bebe?"

"So it is alright if she remains a yokel tied to the land, but not Raghu and Dilip. Is that it? Tell me, who will look after Dilip's parents if we both are not here?"

Ramu scratched his head, thinking up a response.

"Looking after parents is not the only issue. There are many others."

"Tell me, let me also know and understand."

"Lila was very young when we married but she was a cheerful soul, always smiling and giggling, humming songs as she did all the work and went to play with the girls sometimes. Then I went away and got busy with my life. This village is different, so are its people. Once when Lila came, she looked different, her clothes were different, her way of speaking and behaving with people made me ashamed in front of everyone there."

"Maybe when you first went there, you must have been like that too. Everyone says I am like my mother. So perhaps I too will shame you if I come. Even Raghu and Dilip will shame you when they go with you now."

"Change takes time. They'll get used to those ways. But Lila…"he paused for words.

"What about Ma? Why?"

"She was just not comfortable there. It was supposed to be a holiday, but she worried constantly, about Baoji and Bebe, about the village and the *kheti* (farming), about my living in squalor, about the expense, about the next harvest, about so many things. It was so much worry that she forgot how to laugh. Then she wanted to come back. After that, she never came again."

"But you came, once a year. Why didn't you persuade her like you are trying to persuade me?"

The father looked at his hands, then turned them over as if he was examining his nails. He knew what she was asking; he had an answer, but could he give that answer to a young daughter on the threshold of marriage? Shrugging his shoulders he said, "Okay, we'll look out for someone else for you some other time. Stop worrying, nothing will happen to your Ma."

They went back, said nary a word to the questioning faces, but all too soon, the three men were gone. Lila managed a wan smile for Ramu and Raghu; the tears which threatened to spill over were held back by a steely resolve until they were out of sight.

The next time Ramu came back, not in a year's time, but after four short months, a strapping lad in tow. Ramu was expansive on the positives of this match.

"Nimi, he has lived in Nasik all his life. He will not need change; he is like that only. And he wants a bride from the village to bring this flavour into his life. He is a good boy. You will be happy with him and his family there."

This time around, it was Nimi who led her father out of the house. Compassion, shame, anger and so many expressions chased themselves across her face until they reached the glade.

"Why have you brought him? You could have written or sent a photo."

"Don't you like him?"

"That is not the point. I am no burden on you that you're taking such pains to get rid of me."

"Nimi, I want you close to me in the city."

"And Ma? All alone?"

"Nimi, you are at the threshold of life now; think of yourself."

"I am thinking of that too. I will be a stranger in the city. Better that I marry someone here. At least I will not be alone and can be there for Ma, Bebe and Baoji."

"But, your life is your own, not theirs."

"Like yours is your own?"

"Haven't I come for Raghu and you?"

"Yes — after so many years that I wonder why you have remembered us now? us only, not Ma?" Nimi took a deep breath before moving forward, a trifle gingerly. "Bebe told me how Ma changed after her holiday with you. I asked Ma…"

That evoked a sharp reaction. "What did she tell you?"

"Many things. Now I understand some things better. Why she relied so much on Mamaji."

"Don't mention that scoundrel. Why does she rely on him? Why does he avoid me?"

"Whom else could she rely on? She had to learn to read and write along with Raghu and me. You were never there when anything happened — illness, school admissions, exams, harvesting, spraying, marketing, taking loans, anything. Had you been there, she would naturally have turned to you. If," she amended slowly, "you would have been there, she would not have needed to do all that. She would have had time for us and for herself like all other women."

This last came out accusingly, in a rush of youthful fervour.

Nimi had almost come out with the painful secret her mother had confided in her, to warn her against falling into a similar trap. Unconsciously, she echoed her mother's painful recounting.

"You were never here. Always in the city. When she came of age and became the butt of all, who was there to take her side? Bebe only thought of you. The daughter-in-law is always poison. But when her own brother appeared on the scene, that poison became a sweet and she looked conveniently away."

Nimi's tongue stilled as she recalled Lila looking away, pain and wonder chasing across her face.

"What is chastity?" Lila had declaimed. "There is only Maya. (illusion). If anyone looked at me, she used to curse them. But her brother, how could she say anything to him, even when he stole her son's right? She even pretended to lose her old bangle, so he could sell it to take us to a *dai* (midwife) somewhere else far away to clear my womb the first time, as your father had not touched me. The *dai* here would have told the whole village."

"Ma, what about Baba?"

"What about him? He came only once a year and used me for three weeks. That's all. Baoji also accepted the situation, except to keep reminding me that your Baba was my husband. What could I say to him without shattering his ego or his faith in his wife? The rest of the year, here was someone I learnt slowly to rely on, to lean on, and to seek help and advice from.

"We learnt from each other and we taught each other. He taught me about the world outside our village and away from your Baba's Nasik *mohalla*, they call it Peth. I taught him about emotions and relationships and about you children. He never married; and avoids your Baba as far as possible. Why have a confrontation? It's been so many years now. But when your Baba comes, I am always tense. I can't help it. I know that in Nasik, he too…he too…." Lila's voice trailed off.

"How do you know? Did he tell you?" Nimi demanded

"As if anyone would. He was not at ease when I went. Maybe his touch was different. It made me uneasy. I could sense something different when I reached there. The women in the chawl would snigger behind my back; even drop broad hints in front of me. He had taken a room for us but usually he lived in another lane, with a widow who worked in his factory. She was looking after her brother and his children. The women said that sometimes when there was a big order, they had to do overtime or night duty. Then they slept in the factory itself and came home in the morning together."

Lila paused at the memory of the question marks in her mind. "It could have been just her, or so many others. Men need variety, don't they? Especially away from home and no-one to control them. I asked him whom he worked with, but he never took me to meet them, nor to his factory. The thought of it made me uncomfortable, with all the women talking so much about it. I just came back home. Who knows?" Lila ruminated, "the widow may have seen me or someone may have pointed me out. I looked different; that was her home ground — all of them in their graceful nine yard saris, green and red glass bangles, mango shaped nose rings and thick silver toe rings."

Ramu's voice grated on Nimi's reverie. He almost shook the girl.

"What poison, what sweet? What are you talking about? What have Bebe and your Ma done?" He looked at Nimi closely

She collected herself. "Bebe and Ma? What can they do? What can women do, except lie down...." Her voice trailed off.

"Don't change the subject? What have those two told you?"

"Nothing. Only that Ma changed after she visited your city." She looked at her father boldly. "Slowly Ma became more confident. She took control of the farming and she started learning a lot of new things which she never did before."

"And time for herself?" he archly recalled her earlier taunt.

"She gave that up. She became very simple. You have seen that. I think she looks wonderful with just that red bindi and her silver *jhumkas*. Because my Ma is beautiful even without dressing up; with that, she would become Aishwarya Rai. Who wants a mother like that?"

"Look Nimi, if you come to the city, your fate will not be of the women who just lie down. There women do all sorts of work."

"We do it too. Ma and I are not just milking the cows, tending the hens or churning butter. We tend the fields, even drive the tractor. Even Ma used to until Raghu took over. She never wasted money on a driver. Only in the market did she let Mamaji or Raghu do the talking, with her prompting sharply so that we got the best deals. How do you think she brought us up?"

Ramu shook his head to clear his thoughts. All the arguments he had worked on all the way here were gone. What poisoned sweet was Nimi talking about? He too had sensed the changes in Lila, before and after the visit to his city.

In the city she had constantly looked at him speculatively. He felt her eyes on him and an almost desperate wanting to please and satisfy him. It was almost as if she was trying to seduce him back home. And he had been on the edge, fearful that his guilty secret might be out.

When Lila insisted on going home, he was almost relieved. He wanted her gone before any chance meeting could happen. Thoughts slithered in and out of his mind.

'What did Bebe and Lila do? Was it because of me, because I left Lila? I had my new life, peopled by my new family? What did Lila have? How did she manage her life? Did she? Who? Was it really Mama?'

The thoughts plagued Ramu. He thought of asking his mother, but his courage failed him. His guilt was never this heavy in the city. He tried to get through to Lila.

"Talk to Nimi. Tell her they'll both be together with his parents. No question of any separation we have lived through. Lila, she'll listen to you. She worships you."

Lila caught her lip. She got the gist of Ramu's thought process. He did not want his daughter to suffer from those pangs of separation that he had inflicted on his wife.

For a fleeting moment, Lila was mutinous. 'You never thought about my pangs of separation, did you?' she railed mutely. Then the mother in her took over, "Why should my Nimi suffer what I did. That she should go down the road that I have, balancing two lives, satisfying neither."

But Nimi was emphatic. "I will live here only. If all the boys want to go to Nasik, then I'll remain alone here." There were plenty of matches for Nimi – a beautiful educated girl whose father worked in the city. Who did not know how Lila had looked after the farming, her children and her in-laws?

When the marriage took place, Ramu came in a foul mood, which persisted through the festivities, despite Nimi's pleading eyes and smiles. After that it was a long while before they saw him. Only his money orders came now, regular as clockwork, then an ATM card, which Nimi used to draw money when she or Lila needed it.

Several years later, a couple got off the incoming train. The man's looks were familiar. The station master squinted through the bars of the ticket windows, scratching his head in puzzlement. His companion was a total enigma.

The sari that slipped gracefully through her legs showed off not just her full figure but the legs as well. Jingling anklets circled the neat ankles and Kolhapuri chappals encased the slim feet with shining, painted toes. The face was round, as was the bun behind, encircled by a generous string of fragrant white flowers. A huge red bindi with a little black line under it topped the nose, from which dangled a pearl and garnet nose ring.

'Who are they?' wondered the station louts as the couple engaged a porter and started to walk down the long road to the village.

It was only when they were well on their way, with the man pointing out the features to the woman that it hit the station master.

"Ramu — it is Ramu, with a beard and glasses. He is greying. Who is she?" The look of possession between the two had been unmistakable. He dispatched a runner to give the news. The morning peace of the household shattered with the breathless burst: "Ramubabu has reached with a Marathan." (a maharashtran woman)

Baoji recovered first. "Carry on your churning Lila. Let's see what he wants now. Better put some tea on," he instructed his wife. "Are the parathas done?" He was blabbering, worry and joy mingling in his voice.

The tea bubbled, the parathas warm in the cloth lined basket; the churning was the only sound in the waiting courtyard, the old man in his easy chair, the old woman on her cot and Lila squatting on a low stool behind the tall pot she churned after her early morning round of the fields.

The chain clanked loud when Ramu pushed the door open. He stood in the middle of the doorway, taking in the white-washed courtyard, the newly rebuilt kitchen and the solar cooker proudly in front of it. Lila was as usual churning her butter.

Slowly he stepped aside and pulled the Marathan forward. Tension was also writ on her face but she met the scrutiny boldly, seeking Lila's eyes, before she bowed to the old people touching their feet with her folded hands. Tea and breakfast bridged the initial awkwardness.

While the lady went to bathe in the new bathroom recently added inside, Lila called Nimi. "Your Baba has come." She did not mention the guest. It would take Nimi sometime to complete her own household routine and reach home to meet her father.

Meanwhile father and son walked to the glade.

"Baoji, I want to come home. Dilip and Raghu are settled there, but I need my home now." Tears flowed unabashedly down the old wrinkled cheeks.

"There will be problems," Ramu continued, "Lila...."

"What about Lila?" Baoji's tone was sharp, protective.

"I know I am have wronged her. You tell me, what do I do now? If I remain in the city, the wrong continues. But I want to come home. I have responsibilities there too. There is no escape. For me she faced the wrath of her family, her whole neighbourhood, her caste people to marry an outsider." The old man's eyes widened at the word: 'Marry?'

"How could I desert her in Nasik just because I wanted to come back home?"

"You think of yourself always. You wanted to go, you went. You wanted to come back, after years of silence, you came. Did you think of the consequences? You knew your wrong-doing with Lila, but it did not bother you. Now you want to come home to Lila, why bring a Marathan in tow? What are you expecting this time?"

"Why do you think it does not bother me? It does. It bothers her also. That is why she has come with me, to share Lila's burden."

Baoji's eyes narrowed. "Share the burden or the sale of the land?"

It was Ramu's turn to blanch. "Are you selling?"

"Lila will decide."

"What about Raghu? Nimi?"

"Who does the farming? Lila will have to decide. It is her land, her house."

"Your house?"

"No longer. When we needed loans and she had to do all the paper work, it was convenient to put the properties in her name for various loans. Recently some agents came to talk about converting some of the land into a farming hotel."

"Farming hotel? What is that?"

"These *videshis* (foreigners) who come home for a holiday, they want to live on a farm but with hotel facilities. They are interested in the field near the road. They took," the old man bit his tongue, "your Mama abroad for training." Ramu chewed his lip in concentration.

At home, Lila and the Marathan were at it. Lila recalled that she was the widow with whom Ramu lived.

"He felt remorse over leaving you alone. He did not want to repeat it leaving me alone there. That is why he brought me here, that we should all be together."

"If he could leave me alone, why not you?"

"You had the children, Baoji, Bebe."

"And you?"

"Lila," the Marathan took her work hardened hands in hers, "we go back a long way. We could not marry then because I had to not only care for my brother's children, but also arrange their marriages. We were together for years and years, but only got married about five years ago."

'After Nimi,' thought Lila.

"If he had left me to come back home, his reputation would have been muddied. Raghu's would have been affected. And they would have slaughtered me, a widow, remarrying and then being deserted? I would have become a free-for-all. So he brought me here with him."

Lila closed her eyes. 'What now?' she thought, her nebulous dream of selling the land and going away going up in smoke.

"Lila, what are you thinking? Did they not have more than one wife in the olden times? And lived well. We'll share and between us, keep Ramu under control."

"What control, Marathan? I was too young when he first left. But in all these years, have you controlled him? If you had, would he be here to disrupt our lives all over again?" Lila was bitter. "Now, I had learnt to live without him. Why must we begin all over again? Why have you brought him back?"

The Marathan was stunned. Her act of piety in bringing the Prodigal son home had turned sour. "You don't want him here?" suspicions chased through her mind.

'Why? Why did Lila not want Ramu home? Did she have plans of her own?'

The old lady was ecstatic at the return of the Prodigal. She fumed at Lila.

"See we have won. He has come back. What more do you want?"

Lila blazed back, "Am I a button to be switched on and off or a plate to be passed around?" The Marathan did not follow that exchange.

As the men walked in, the old woman welcomed her son gleefully. No-one echoed her happiness. The consequences were too ominous. Tension clouded the homecoming.

Initially the Marathan stayed aloof but wary of Lila. She watched her routinely intently. Then suddenly, one day, no one knew why, she collapsed at Lila's knees.

"Lila Didi I know you have been wronged. Your life has been a hard one. But listen to mine." Lila shrugged her off.

"What does it have to do with me?" she turned to the small window behind her.

The Marathan kept at it. "Didi, around the time you got married to Ramu, I was widowed. I don't even remember seeing my husband. My brother took me away from my in-laws' beatings, to look after his ailing wife. After she died, I brought up his children and worked in the factory. My life was divided between the home and the factory. For years Ramu and I bickered. We were like children. One day when he was ill, I looked after him and after that, things changed between us. But will people allow a widow any happiness? Whether it is the caste panchayat or the peth committee, there is little difference. When we promised him we would not marry until all his children were settled, my brother finally let a room to Ramu. Slowly the whole peth (community) accepted him. Then he brought Dilip and Raghu. They are good boys."

Lila turned. "So you have taken my Raghu also."

"Not taken. He is not my son Didi. Let him be our son. See, if Ramu had left me there when he wanted to come home, he would have compounded his sin of leaving you. Don't you see that? You had Baoji and Bebe to back you. But had Ramu deserted me, my brother would have been no armour for me — a remarried deserted, widow. They would have sold me, not to the highest bidder, but to every bidder, even those who would not have paid. You are a woman. Think what would have been my fate if Ramu did not bring me with him."

"So he brought you. What do you want of me now? You are his wife, you say. So go to him."

"He needs you to understand."

"Understand what? Okay, go and tell him I have understood his needs. Tell me Marathan, you plead so eloquently for his needs. What about my needs?" Lila bit her tongue sharply.

"We will all be together."

"So?" Lila said archly. The Marathan was silent. She knew her answer. But Ramu's?

Lila had something else on her mind. She thought of the

real estate agent who had talked to her and Mama — the nebulous plans, the chance of getting away – all slipping away. She turned her back on the Marathan to grip the thick bars of her window looking out onto the mango tree in the backyard.

'This cage is like a prison. Its hold never loosens,' she thought.

Nimi had come and gone. While she was there, her father and his new wife hung around her, pampering her. She could only sneak a few moments alone with her mother, "Be careful Ma. This longing for home all of a sudden? There's something more to it. For God's sake, don't sign any papers for anybody."

The land and the house had been in Lila's name for a long long time now, in fact since soon after she took over the farming. But it never weighed as heavy as it did now, with the question marks in everyone's eyes.

Since Ramu and his wife showed up, Mama had made himself scarce. There was no one she could talk to. Even Nimi was running scared. Her in-laws asked pointed questions as the word spread.

"Tell me, Marathan," queried Lila, "why did you decide to come to this village?"

"Because it is Ramu's."

"Why did Ramu decide to come back for good? He had a good job. Why did he give it up? For what?"

"What good job? Who wants old people? The factory was going to be changed in some ways. They told all of us to take a lump sum and go because we would not be able to handle the new machines."

"So you both got lump sums. Why the village? You could have lived on in Nasik."

"Didi, with that money? It would barely buy a small room far from the city."

"What about your house?"

"First we lived in my brother's house. Then when his sons married and had children, we moved out to our own room. But the landlord had been after us to vacate, as rents had gone up and so had the *pagri* (the initial deposit)."

"So?"

"Ramu told him that we would stay or sublet. So the landlord agreed to give us a lump sum to move out."

"So you have that money also...."

"Yes, Ramu decided to come home. Here that money would mean a very comfortable life as there is already a home and farming."

Bebe's eyes narrowed as she took in this news. Lila mulled over it too, wondering why Ramu had not mentioned it at all. She wondered what Bebe would tell Baoji. Had Ramu confided in his father? Should she talk it over with the old man?

Her dilemma stood. Obviously the old people would

lean towards their son. All said and done, Lila, despite all her slogging over the years, was their daughter-in-law, an outsider, wasn't she?

"That they look to me for a lead, are waiting for me to decide, is big enough itself. How long before they demand their land and house back? What will become of me then?" Lila voiced these fears to Nimi whom she met in the fields in private.

"Where is Raghu?" demanded Nimi. "Ma, have they mentioned him at all in all this? Where is he living if Baba has given up his house?" Mother and daughter reached home in a quandary.

"Baba," demanded Nimi after the greetings, "Where is Raghu? You haven't told me anything about him. What is he doing? Is he earning well or is it still hand-to-mouth?" This arch comment was vintage Nimi.

"Raghu is in Dubai," Ramu announced. "He got a good offer. We paid a lump sum to the agent to send him there."

Lila flew off the handle. "Dubai? You sent my son across the seas without even telling us; and through an agent. Don't you know how these agents fleece the money and then consign them to living hells in foreign countries; and that only if they somehow manage to survive the illegal journey? Have you no sense of shame left or has Nasik drained it all?"

All her pent up frustrations were bursting out with her wild accusations. "First you went off to find yourself another wife. Then you took my son and lost him for me. Thank God Nimi did not fall for your sweet talk, otherwise who knows where you would have sold her off."

"Hold your tongue. Don't you dare accuse me...?"

"That I will. Tell me what I have said wrong. Did you not go off leaving me to care for your parents and your land? Did you even bother about anything, but your factory and your Marathan? When Raghu was old enough to earn for you, you took him off with you. Had Nimi not put her foot down, you would have done the same to her. Now you have come back with your compensation money which you told no one about, to live off the fat of the land. The house is there and so is the farm. Lila *kaam karegi aur hum aish karenge* (Lila will work and we will enjoy). Take your wife and go back to where you came from."

Those ominous words, which had hung overhead for so long, were out!

Even as Lila felt the relief of uttering what had been festering inside, she felt Baoji advising restraint with his bony hand on her shoulder.

Ramu, who had barely spoken to Lila since he came, lashed back.

"This is my home, my land, my village, my farm, my parents. I live here as a matter of right, under my father's roof. Who are you to tell me to go?"

This was a red flag to a raging bull. Lila planted her hands on her hips and Nimi stationed herself firmly by her side.

"You want to know who I am. Let me tell you Nasikwale Babu Ramuji; I am the owner of this house and this farm. There are legal papers to prove it. You may be Baoji, Bebe's son and the pitiable father of Raghu and Nimi. But you have been neither son, nor father, nor husband in any true sense. I have looked after them since I was less than ten years old. I know every detail of their requirements and what has to be done to keep them alive. In you or your Marathan's hands, they would be dead in less than a month. Is that what you want now?"

"Lila, Raghu has only gone to Dubai. That is not the end of the world. He is making good money."

"So good that you could retire from your job but keep it hidden from all of us? In case we snatch the money? Is that why?"

"You are determined to misunderstand. Why are you doing this?"

"You tell me, why are you doing this? Why have you come? Tell everyone the full truth. What else have you hidden from us?"

Tension thick enough to cut with a knife hung over the house waiting for Ramu's answer. It was obvious that the issue could only be resolved by Ramu and Lila, but neither would speak.

Baoji led Lila to the glade.

"Beti, how long can we live with this tension? What are you thinking? What do you want?"

"Peace, Baoji, some peace that these two have snatched from us."

"It is his home after all." (Ah! she thought, it is coming out now).

"Not mine?"

"Beti, yours too. Yours too. But — was it like this when you went there?"

"I never met her; but yes, something from the way the women spoke; who knows, they may have told me but I didn't understand them then."

"Tell me, what should we do now?"

"Baoji, what is there to do? Your son created this situation years ago and now he wants all the *malai*, (the cream). Why is he pestering you to transfer the house and farm to him when he already has all his money and Raghu's and no will to work the land?"

"If it is plonked on his shoulders, he will have to work it."

"*Arre mere bhole* Baoji (Oh! My simple father). With his Marathan to encash it? Let me tell you, here and now, whether I stay here or not, I will not sign the house or the land over to him. It will remain in my name till I die and then it will be Nimi's. Who knows one day it will be her only pillar as it is mine today. Your son will never get it."

"Lila beti, where will you go?"

"Let me think about it. It is a big world."

"Why not live together in peace?"

"Did I disrupt the peace? Your son did. Why don't you talk to him to get the truth of his intentions out of him and his Marathan?"

One morning the old people woke up to the loss of Lila. When she did not come back from the fields at her usual time, the Marathan bestirred herself to deal awkwardly with the household chores. Baoji set off in search. Lunch was sombre and then Baoji called Nimi from Ramu's mobile.

"Ma said she was going away for some time. Let them cope with the ploughing and seeding."

Ramu shouted exasperatedly, "This is the busy season and the land agents are coming next week."

"Baoji," said Nimi, "tell him to get to work and leave the agents to Ma and Mamaji."

Ramu let out a lewd curse. His daughter spoke, "Don't forget that in our childhood, he was the father we never had and he has paid for it with exile."

It was a transformed Lila who returned weeks later. Gleaming and sleek in an expensive sari, manicured hands and feet, a chic short hairdo and a trendy purse slung on her shoulder; she walked, nay glided in, albeit a bit awkwardly, trailed by Nimi. Bowing to Baoji and Bebe, she glanced at the Marathan, pointedly ignoring Ramu.

"Baoji it is all fixed. I have started my training for the

farming hotel. Nimi will follow so we can run it together. The company is paying for the training and for setting up the hotel but the land will remain in my name only. Profits will be shared."

"Listen to this fool woman. Whoever heard of such a silly scheme? What if…?"

Lila ignored him. "Baoji, the lawyers are drawing up the papers and Nimi's husband and Mamu have talked to the lawyers; if your son cannot manage this season, we can hire a temporary local manager. Don't worry. Once the training is over and the hotel organized, between us, Nimi and I will manage the hotel and the farming. Just don't bother about him."

Ramu sputtered at Nimi's chin thrust in his direction. The old people's eyes were wet, Ramu was venomously baleful and the Marathan worried.

"Where are you living, Lila?" Bebe was anxious.

"In the training hostel. Once the hotel is ready, I will go there and Nimi will go for training."

"When will you come home?"

"Here? For what? Don't worry, Nimi and I will bring your medicines and other things."

"But?"

The Marathan leapt forward and grasped Lila's hands. "Didi, I did not come here to drive you from your home."

Lila grasped her by the shoulders and gave her a little

shake. "It is my home. I will come and go as I please. You have no say in it. You tell us, why did you come? For what?"

The Marathan turned to look helplessly back at Ramu's blank stare.

"Go on, tell us what you came for… no? So let me tell them. I have been hearing all that is being discussed outside these four walls. You came to sell off all the land and leave Baoji, Bebe and me in this little house to survive with whatever you two chose to send us. Nimi is in her home and Raghu is far away, sending you money every month. You went to Western Union to collect it last week, didn't you?"

Ramu gave a furious glare and the Marathan blanched. At the gasp of the old people, Lila turned to them

"Yes, the plan was to sell off all the land so now your son can turn from a factory labourer into a big businessman in his old age. That is why I refused to sell even that one roadside field. All the land will remain in my name. And," turning sharply to the other two," it will be no use killing me off either. My will has been left with a good lawyer who knew my father. He will never let you get your hands on the land or this house."

Ramu was truly unmanned and it showed. "Mama" he finally burst out.

Lila rained scorn on him. "I have concerns other than those of the body. Are you going to cry about milk which was spilt decades before you brought your wife here so shamelessly? Your Mama went to America long ago and will never come back. Yes, he is in touch with Nimi and guided us about the hotel, the lawyers, everything from there. How do you think the agents found our land only in this whole village? There are other roadside fields also. Had you not come back with your Marathan, Baoji, Bebe and I may have seen America too. But maybe it is in your fate to always be a spoiler of lives. Who can fight fate?"

Quickly embracing the elders, Lila walked swiftly out.

Que Sera Sera

'Ye Gods! Is this what becomes of longtime NRIs? Or is my sister special?' the thought chased through Pallavi's stunned mind. 'What's happened to this girl?'

She was receiving her NRI sister Vrinda and was horrified at the weight she had put on — multiple chins, rolls of fat and lots of make-up. Looking at her manly shoes, she thought: 'Must get her some decent pairs of Louboutin soon.'

As soon as they made themselves comfortable in the car, the younger sister took off her shoes to show off her exquisitely moulded feet and painted toes, to wink wickedly at Pallavi:

"Drives 'em nuts. Watch these sexy feet emerge from those boots, after checking out these luscious lips and generous breasts, panting for what's between the legs…" Vrinda purred sexily.

Pallavi blanched. Vrinda giggled: the chauffer's neck was reddening.

"Pallo, you were not like this. Has marriage done this? Then, I'm glad that for me, Pa answered that famous Ad for a Green Card Professional. See the freedom it gave me."

They tacitly agreed to stop at a coffee bar to exchange personal confidences before reaching home.

"What actually happened to you? You never wrote about the divorce; thereafter all those men. I did not want to broach the subject in their presence when I was there."

"The old Pallavi tact coming to the fore. For Pa and Ma anyway, it was best that they died so soon after my wedding. They never knew who they got me married to."

Pallavi shot up an eyebrow. "The green card professional, handsome, five-figure salary, own house, etc."

"Yes dear, you must remember the quick engagement followed by a quicker wedding. They were so thrilled, so was I and my in-laws." The younger sister was eager to get it off her chest finally.

Vrinda's Tale: A Green Card Alimony

"That first week after the wedding in India I almost went crazy trying to seduce my handsome husband, but no go. Rajiv didn't touch me on the first night — obviously it was too late and both of us dead beat. The next night he was sozzled; the third he spent with his Dad till I fell asleep and the fourth with his buddies for a delayed stag party. The next the whole family stayed up catching up because we were to leave the next day, so, I reached the great U S of A a virgin... a bloody god-damned married eight days virgin! And you'll never guess the next....

"At the airport, I was received by my husband's Husband!

"Rajiv was gay. That handsome hulk, the professional Green Card holder was a homosexual and his parents had never guessed!"

Pallavi gasped aloud.

"Actually he let me off quite gently, explaining that he owed it to his parents and that to make sure I got something out of it, he promised not to divorce me until I got my Green Card, which should take long enough to establish my credentials back home for having tried to save the marriage.

"I thought to myself, 'what a mess, with me dying to try out sex.' Question was with whom? Seeing those two guys billing and cooing to make up for the three week absence drove me up the wall, and set me off on a wild goose chase. Almost like nymphomaniac, I ran through boyfriends. Took six months of awful sex to surface and take stock of the mess in my life.

"I couldn't write home — it would have been too much for Pa-ma and terrible for Rajiv; he was actually quite a decent sort, even moved heaven and earth for my Green Card. People offer green cards in dowry, I got mine in alimony! He gave me back every penny Pa had spent on our wedding, the clothes, jewellery, everything. Then he got me married and his husband gave me away — it was quite amusing."

Looking back on those times, her voice softened:

"It was too late. Something was gone from inside me. I just let the guys slip through my fingers, running through boyfriends, lovers, husbands – only two things kept me going, work, work and work and no kids to mess up the break-ups."

The outpouring seemed to purge her, as if by confessing, she had dipped in the proverbial Ganga. Vrinda took huge gasps of air and pushed aside the now-cold coffee, "Now you know about my past, let me unravel your present."

Pallavi's Present: A Showcase For A Living Doll

The gate was imposing enough, elaborately ornate, iron black, with a tall pole holding aloft a brass bell of the type found in smaller temples and a colourful plaited bell pull. Before Vrinda finished wondering whether the sound would actually carry into the house, she was inside the gate and letting out a gasp of pleasure.

It was a sight for sore eyes and vintage Pallavi — obviously age had not withered her talent for creating niches of beauty around herself, nor had money coarsened her taste.

Pallavi collected her antiques and also used them well. The lawn was large with borders adorned with artfully placed artefacts interspersed with obviously expensive well-tended plants — a carved elephant here, a robust horse there, a svelte lady with her mates opposite.

A tiny pond boasted of a single lotus, fronting the last step of a miniature temple atop a mini hill, backed by large umbrella palms that screened off the sights of peeping toms next door.

Vrinda recognized the locality, monopolized by Old Money, where land was priced sky-high. Selling out was sacrilege; commuting from the new villa and farmhouse colonies totally down-market. So what could the poor rich people do, but add value to their over-priced properties?

The marble walk ended on a marble veranda, if it could be called that, the entrance dominated by a Nandi bull sitting square in the middle, looking into a large hall. On one side a stately staircase led up to a landing fronting a set of rooms which ringed one large area of the hall. The arrangement was obviously replicated from the other side of the massive room, allowing another gallery of suites to overlook the other half. All very, very elegant, very, very old and luxuriously expensive.

Vrinda sat pondering, waiting for sleep.

Dinner had been a sombre affair; her famous brother-in-law, a tiger of the business world, turned out to be a taciturn man, as spare of word as he was of frame. Greying fashionably at the temples, well turned out, courteous but silent.

'Was it disapproval?' Vrinda wondered.

The heaviness he generated was anathema to his father, a charming urbane host, with a twinkle in his eye, as he sparred humorously with the sisters. The affection for his daughter-in-law was unmistakable. After dinner, Pallavi had taken his arm and led him into the garden for his 'constitutional'.

Vrinda declined. "Let me get to know my brother-in-law", she had said, not quite knowing what she had let herself in for. Later she was to conclude, 'this marriage has only survived because of the old man', as she sat delving into her old family knowledge.

Pallavi was several years her senior. At 18, she had made a brilliant match, doing her middle class parents proud. Vrinda had been still at school when Pallavi finished with her childbearing at 21, with another milestone, the family heir and his sister.

Now, she was a classy mother-in-law, the epitome of ageing with grace. Over the years, her looks had matured and she had apparently learnt to cultivate a style all her own.

Society magazines had made legends of her sari and jewel collections, invitations to her parties were sought after and the house was the subject of photo features. All of which was very nice, but for that shadow behind the smile in her eyes when she countered her father-in-law's sallies. When she came to show Vrinda her bedroom, she could not resist asking, "God, Pallavi, how can you stand it?"

"What?"

"The Sphinx... I tried every trick in the book to talk to your husband," Vrinda threw her hands up in the air expressively. Pallavi's only reply was a slight movement of her head and a tiny smile, half humorous, half ironic, as she let herself quietly out of the room.

Awaiting sleep, Vrinda heard the two distinct wings of the house — one settling down to sleep as the mistress sent in glasses of saffron and almond-flavoured milk to the bedrooms and the other, where young people were enjoying an evening of music.

"That is our Mastani room," the old man told her. In deference to her raised eyebrow, he explained, "Mastani was the second wife of Peshwa Baji Rao I. Her palace was remarkably resurrected at the Kelkar Museum after the palace burnt down. Pallavi spent hours in the museum and then recreated it with some design changes for our musical evenings."

When she peeked in the next day, Vrinda saw the music parlour, divided into two sections by a semi-circular, low, carved screen, barely a foot high, and waxed almost black. It separated the generous enclosure for the performers from the seating for the audience.

'Pallavi has learnt the lessons of wealth well', thought Vrinda, noting the pristine white of the fluffed pillows and bolsters, a quick and efficient change from the merrymaking into the wee hours.

Confidences

Vrinda saw a new sister. The convent educated lass had made a remarkable changeover from Indian English to chaste Hindi and even Urdu; philosophy, yoga, meditation, even *riyaz* (practise) with a music teacher, learned discussions and chess with her father-in-law who apparently escorted her to seminars and workshops, in between preparing for the next party.

But something was wrong. What?

Vrinda could not quite put her finger on it. Her relations were warm, even with her son and daughter-in-law, the Sphinx supremely indifferent to all, especially Pallavi's ironic sallies.

"Show me those famous collections."

Pallavi led her into her suite, another miniature haveli, executed in soothing pastels, carved *jharokhas*, and priceless artefacts.

A thought distracted her from the collection.

"Tell me, how does the Sphinx fit in here?"

"Where?"

"In this room, I mean. Isn't it too feminine for him?"

"This is mine. His is down the corridor."

"Really Pallavi — separate bedrooms. Since when?"

"I took this over when my ma-in-law died and naturally

did it over completely."

"What about Pa?"

"He has his own next door, between yours and mine."

"Runs in the family, — does your daughter-in-law also...?"

"Not yet, but who has seen the future?"

"But why? It can't be his silences, can it...after all you have had two kids, haven't you?"

Pallavi tried to brush the question away. What had made her change her mind, that fateful day?

"We last went to bed together when I conceived Mini. The kids ended our relationship." The silence became pregnant. "Sujoy is what I call negative religious."

She answered the question on her sister's face, "What I call positive religion is that which brings, if not happiness, at least peace, a joy, a celebration in the creations of God, a helping hand, a lightness of spirit; it is not necessary that one be overflowing with the milk of human kindness.

"My mother-in-law's brand of religion was the negative one. Fasts, prayers, penance for all worldly joys — even for conjugal relations. Can you beat that? That was only necessary for procreation — she taught him that and he learnt those lessons well.

"As soon as I became pregnant, I was shifted to her dark sombre rooms, with their *diya-battis* day and night. My only escape was going home for the confinement and she prolonged that till Munna was almost eight months.

"After that the dictum was, 'no sex as long as you are breastfeeding.' Munna was a year old when she lifted her ban. Then, first time unlucky, I got pregnant and was back to square one. That pregnancy was difficult enough for me to hate him for abandoning me to the tender mercies of his mother.

"That pure white organdie," she pondered, "hid a spiteful heart. She loved her son to distraction and hated all the rest of us, her husband, her daughters and her daughter-in-law, for distracting from his "Glory" — What was he beyond an efficient money-making machine? If he had to select his own wardrobe, he would be on the worst dressed list."

"Then?" prompted the younger sister breathlessly, absorbing a new side of her Pallo.

"Mini was breastfed for almost three years. Then one day, I read somewhere that women," a broad smile broke out over Pallavi's nostalgia, "with high fever should avoid feeding their babies. Can you imagine my excitement — swiping a cut onion from the kitchen from under her beady eyes; I wrapped it in half a dozen hankies to smother the smell, carted it around until I could safely tuck it into my armpit and then walked around for what seemed like hours on the sunniest footpaths to work up a temperature! I was so disgusted with myself that day, for being such a healthy cow. When the temperature was raging, I headed home, but she caught me at the stairs and it was no go. I had to wait for my next period, have the ritual bath after five days and then only would I be allowed to 'pollute' my husband. Madam's orders..." she threw up her hands recalling the bygone despair.

"Now I too learnt to be devious. This time, I waited beyond her prescribed five days. On the seventh day, Sujoy was due back from a business trip and I was not on hand at home to receive him. I spent the day shopping for a new sari to wear after a full day in the parlour making myself over — the works, body massage, henna, facial, treatments, make-up, everything."

"Wow!"

"Just you wait. He was in the study with his father when I reached home and I literally sneaked into the house and straight into my room, to avoid bumping into her. He came in, a good two hours later... Two long hours with me on tenterhooks you can only imagine; and then...." she paused and the anguish of the recollection flashed across her expressive face.

Rejection

"What are you doing here?" Sujoy demanded.

"I live here; it's my room too, isn't it?" Pallavi replied with a quick nervous smile as she approached him, hands outstretched. Quickly, before she could lose her nerve, she wound her hands around his neck and smiled shyly up at him.

But before she could go any further, he plucked off the offending arms with two disapproving fingers each and returned them to her side.

"I don't like or believe in this nonsense. We've got two children, no more. I can't afford to waste any more time and energy on doing extra pooja or penance instead of running my business."

Pallavi was completely stunned, unable to comprehend what exactly Sujoy meant.

"What do you want me to do?"

"Everything. Look after the kids, help Amma with the house, do your pooja, whatever — only don't bother me with this sex nonsense. I want none of it."

"But – but – What?"

Sujoy cut in, "No buts and whats. You are my wife, mother of my children, daughter-in-law of my parents — to the end of your days. Only no more sex for us. It's too unclean. We have done our duty for the family by producing heirs — now no more," he stressed the point as he stalked off to the dressing room to change and then promptly and peacefully fell asleep.

Pallavi picked up her tale sombrely. "Can you imagine my state — first a stunned silence, then oceans of tears; by morning I was at his feet, begging: where had I gone wrong? But he was cold. He called in his mother to read me a lecture on morals, wifely duty to follow hubby's dictats and the virtues of abstention etc.

"I don't even remember what else, I was so stupefied; I was reduced to a zombie wasting away in this very house with no life, no identity, no purpose, nothing but a flitting shadow...." She was lost for sometime in traumatic memories of her ultimate rejection.

"Then?" came the prompt, "something, someone must have brought about this transformation. You hardly look like a frustrated, sex-starved, teenage widow. Was it a lover, or lovers plural?"

"One."

"How long?"

"Many, many years."

"No-one ever found out — friends, servants, kids, hubby dear, mother-in-law, someone?"

"We were very discreet, the circumstances were such. Couldn't afford to be found out and then things also worked out right. Sometimes though, I wonder whether Mini has at least suspected. If so, has she discussed it with anyone? Sometimes, I see that query in her eyes, but she never broached the subject and I have held my peace. Why spoil their relationship with their father?"

"No-one ever saw or noticed the difference in you? Your being, your personality, everything?"

"Of course, the changes were evident. I learnt, at times painfully, to withdraw from all other personal relationships.

It was dangerous ground. Either way, I had no words to explain my actions or my motives to anyone, did I?"

"How did it start, where did you meet him, who is he, what is he like, was he married, his wife...?"

A serene smile lit up Pallavi's face. "He is the complete man — a wonderful person, so vital, so alive, so knowledgeable, easy to talk to, to laugh with, and to learn from.

"He has taught me everything that I am today; turned my convent education around on its head and introduced me to Sanskrit, Hindi, Urdu, even French — to religion, philosophy and art. Made me read and meditate, explore the world and the depths of myself to develop my own personality and to step out of the shadows, to take charge of my life. He used to tease me that he had converted me into an Indian."

"How did you meet — where?"

"He just came upon me one day, drooping in my room, weeping as usual with no explanation for it. Somehow, he understood. No words were required, perhaps because of his shrivelled up wife. He just took me into his arms to comfort me and that spark was lit. We couldn't help ourselves; both of us were so starved."

"Here, in this room?"

"No, in that one, Sujoy's. I was still there then, this one came much later."

"Then he was a known person, familiar enough to enter

the family apartments?"

"Of …" Pallavi checked herself. "Yes, yes, he was."

"Then...?"

"What can I tell you? It was such a wonderful release from a grey prison, a relief to get it out, to talk about it, one normal person to another. Of course, we were very careful about synchronizing ourselves with the old lady's satsang sessions, and temple going; but then it was not only sex. We went to other temples, museums and palaces in the cause of my re-education."

"For how long?"

"For months and months. I don't know how long."

"How could you manage it?" she started skeptically and then tuned into a new line of thought, "even now?"

"Of course not, not at this age. Sex is over now. But that affection, love and trust doesn't just go away like that, does it? It continues to mellow and mature and to give perhaps even greater little pleasures."

"You mean to tell me that this paragon just stopped having you and went off, out of your life just like that? Not taking a thing to clear off? What sort of a man was he?"

"You said it; a paragon, but fortunately, he is not out of my life. It slowed down gradually, but we still look after each other."

"No-one ever saw you or suspected a thing?"

"My mother-in-law...."

Vrinda pounced "What about her?"

"She caught us red-handed."

Vrinda let out a low wolf whistle "And in all these years, she did not breathe a word because she had stopped your husband from f**king you? I like that for irony."

"Not at all. It wasn't that way. Actually, for all her mean ways, she was, in her own way, a pious soul. She really believed that sex was evil, a sin."

Pallavi was suddenly quite grave as she recalled the past.

"She must have been stunned when she walked in on us on that fateful day — struck dumb — actually physically dumb. She had a stroke and couldn't speak for some time. Her eyes used to haunt me, made us feel guilty as Hell.

"For her, it must have been the worst possible retribution. How sins catch up with us? After all that raving and ranting about sex, being unable to rail against me or to tell her beloved son — that was the worst possible punishment that could have been inflicted on her."

"I'll bet. That bitch knew all the moves. So that is how she broke it up?" Vrinda demanded.

"Not at all. Somehow, she managed to convey it to her beloved son before she died. Immediately after the ceremonies, he let fly. All the *gaalis* (foul words) on record, good, bad, indifferent, all the adjectives in the bad dictionary, he just pounded away at me. But strangely, the more Sujoy railed, the less guilty I felt; the calmer I became."

Standing Ground

Then it was Pallavi's turn to speak, to refuse to bear his load of shit or guilt.

"After all it was your mother's fault," she threw back at him. "Had she not twisted your mind, we could have been a normal couple and this situation would never have arisen. What has been taken from you that was actually yours? Nothing."

Pallavi bore his name, lived under his roof, ate off his table, ran his home, entertained his associates, and raised his kids, even slept in his bed. He did not want either her love or her body —- had rejected both outright, so why crib if someone else appreciated them.

"Be happy," she threw the words at him, "that I have been careful enough not to have you declared a cuckold publicly."

At that, he almost had an apoplexy and for a moment, Pallavi was scared. Then he stabilized and she saw his eyes narrowing in calculation, thinking perhaps of how he could benefit from the situation. The realization was an ice cold shower over her heated brain.

Pallavi decided there and then that she too would benefit from this situation; everyone would, including her children. With her life at stake, she learnt quickly to drive a bargain. Sujoy was firm.

"No divorce. I will not be humiliated in public; my mother must not be besmirched."

"Fine," Pallavi parried, "no divorce, but I will not live at your mercy either. No blackmail please. I want an independent income at my disposal, from outside your business, in case you run that into the ground."

That was a terrible blow to his ego. "And no more living frugally in this glorified hut. If you want me to continue to be merely your living doll for show, then build a suitable showcase for that doll."

She wrenched from him promise of funds for the renovation of the entire estate, annual holidays for herself and the children, their boarding schools (so that they would not come across the truth), wardrobes, the works.

Only one ground rule: you lead your life, I lead mine, but no-one must know that I am nothing except your biggest social asset.

Retribution

"He didn't touch him?" breathed the astounded listener

"He couldn't. Not in a thousand years. All he did, all he was concerned about was to extricate total power to run the business as he thought fit. Suited us just fine. He ran the business as he thought fit and we ran our lives as we thought fit.

"I moved out of his room into this suite, my erstwhile mother-in-law's abode. It almost killed him to see me do it over, but I stood my ground.

"But believe me, it was as if a heavy yoke had been lifted from our shoulders. As Sujoy got used to the situation, for the first time, I could afford to be seen with him as my official escort in lieu of a husband who was too busy making money.

"For the first time, I took the kids for a holiday and he was there too. Later we went abroad, lots of places where I picked up some of these beauties you see scattered around the house.

"We became regulars on the seminar circuits, learning about all sorts of things, meeting people, making contacts that Sujoy often derived benefit from. But they were," her tone became poignant, "always only contacts, not friends, never friends. That was one luxury neither of us could afford."

"That twinge of guilt was always there at the bottom of our hearts. But Sujoy's distaste was always so comically apparent at home and so dispassionately disguised in company that it gave us a perverse sort of pleasure in flaunting and in tweaking his tail when he was helpless to react in public," she ended with a mischievous chortle.

"How did it end then?" Vrinda asked.

"It didn't. How do normal couples grow old? They just get more used to each other, know each other in and out, generally slow down and then a new pattern of life is set, with new fragrances which linger on...."

"But this was different."

"Not that different actually. Ok, so we did not take

those marriage vows with each other or produce Munna and Mini, but everything else was our joint venture, even raising the kids to whom he is more a father than their biological one; he even helped with the planning of those fabulous monthly parties on which Sujoy places such a business success premium."

"Does Sujoy know that?"

"What?"

"That his rival, or whatever he would be called, is planning his parties?"

"There's little he can do about it, without getting egg on his face; and he really wants to remain on that Best Party list, and wine and dine the rich and the mighty to sell his big dirty deals."

Hours later, Vrinda retired, still puzzling over some missing link, which seemed to be just there, out of her reach....

'What sort of a guy was this?' She thought. 'His whole life spent with another's wife, helping her to entertain her husband's guests. What was the deal, always hiding, never able to acknowledge each other out in the open? Why?'

The riddle wouldn't let her sleep — who, who, who...?

She recounted all that Pallavi had told her — her husband's rejection, the despair, coming out of it in the arms of a lover who moved in and out of her house and apartments without evoking any suspicion, for months on end! How could that be possible even given the large establishment.

The mystery was curdling her brains, repelling sleep.

After sometime, she heard her brother-in-law mount the stairs. Firm hard footfalls marked his progress down the landing to a door down the corridor which opened and then clicked smartly shut.

After a longish spell came the muffled murmurs as her sister came upstairs, no doubt holding her father-in-law's arm after their constitutional walk in the open. Another door opened and clicked shut, next door.

A little later, unrest made Vrinda throw back her covers.

Who could it be, WHO?

She tapped softly at Pallavi's door, determined to talk to her, get it out of her — no response; she let herself in softly, "Are you awake, Pallo?"

A single-shaded light cast its pale circle on the mirror through the open door of the dressing room. The images in the mirror transfixed the intruder.

Vrinda turned her face around to the open connecting door between the suites and the bed beyond. Tiptoeing silently forward, the eavesdropper strained to listen in.

Vrinda couldn't catch a word, but the tender look on her sister's face, the gentle touch of her hand on the weathered cheek below it and the adoration in the eyes of the man were words enough.

'Well said Pallo — old love does not just go away or die out, its fragrance lingers on.'

The Stalked

First day

Madhu stepped out of the office into the fresh air. As she breathed, she immediately felt the difference between the fresh air diluted with petrol fumes and the musty dank smog of the office insides.

She set off at her usual brisk pace; after a while she slowed to step aside, looking around carefully but couldn't pin down the source of her unease: despite her usual total cover-up outfit, there was a prickly sensation between the shoulders and tension in the small of her back. Was someone following her?

Day Two

On the way to the office she was wary, recalling the previous day's unease. She almost sniffed the air, testing it – for what? She didn't know what she was looking for. But the question preoccupied her and before she knew it, she had reached office.

That same uneasy sensation filled her when she left in the evening. She pulled her dupatta wrap closer. Madhu paused deliberately at a mirror panel in a shop window to scan the crowd behind her. Was her anxious look a giveaway?

'I'm watching too many crime serials these days,' she reproved herself. Nevertheless, that uncanny feeling and the tension in the small of her back persisted all the way home.

Day Three

Shortly before she reached the bus stop from home, Madhu felt that same prickly sensation. She had selected a hooded jacket to go over her kurta.

'What now?' she thought, uneasily scanning the crowd of the usual college and office goers. Before leaving office that evening, she scolded herself, 'No more paranoia'. But that did not stop the now familiar prickle that appeared behind her neck and back as she strode to the bus stop.

'I must be going nuts,' she told herself; but was sobered by the realization that the feeling persisted all the way home. By now it was becoming a recognizable sensation; how could she overlook it after Shirley's comments?

College mates — they had graduated, landed their first jobs and then even married at the same time. At lunch time, she beckoned Madhu over in the canteen.

"Who's the old faithful?"

"What old faithful?"

"The guy who's following you around?"

Madhu looked around anxiously.

"Not here stupid. On the way to and from office."

The colour fled from Madhu's cheeks. "Who is he?"

"That's what I asked you," Shirley reminded her.

"Search me. What does he look like?"

"Can't tell. He's always muffled up in a coat with a hat to add to the cover up. What have you done to attract those fake CID types?"

Madhu mulled over that all afternoon. When she stepped out of office, her face was a study in tension. But she couldn't spot the 'fake CID type' anywhere around. Deliberately, she chose a seat at the back of the bus and was the last to alight at her stop. No sign of Mr 'fake CID', except that familiar prickle at the back of her neck as she walked home.

As she approached the front door, suddenly she swung around. A hat loomed in view, several yards away. Madhu panicked and rushed headlong into the house, breathing heavily. Luckily no one noticed as she made straight for her room. That night, she slept badly.

Day Four

No special effort was needed to miss her bus; she hitched a ride from her brother. On the way back, she stuck consciously to the crowd right up to the bus stop. Inside, she sat at the back and screened all the incoming passengers while glancing over her shoulder often at the traffic following her bus to Jangpura. She spotted three hats on scooters, but all too far away to see their faces.

Stepping down, Madhu bumped – thankfully — into a neighbour to chat all the way home. Twice she looked over her shoulder, but her companion's demand for attention was persistent. The slight glimpse of a hat did leave Madhu shaken and sleepless, wondering what to do: confide in her brother? 'It would only worry Ma,' she thought and decided to give it another day.

Day Five

There should have been no question of waiting and watching. There was a muffled hat and coat standing just across from the bus stop in the morning, glimpsed in the passing as she got into the bus. But in the evening, there he was, bold as brass, as she headed towards the bus stop.

Madhu blanched and stopped dead in her tracks so suddenly that the person behind crashed into her, almost sending her sprawling.

Rohan, a colleague, caught hold of her, "Watch out

Madhu. What happened?" He noticed her shaking hands, "What's wrong? You're not looking too good."

"Rohan," she gasped, "a favour please – come with me please...."

"Where to?"

In response, Madhu clutched his hand and rushed headlong into the waiting bus and held on till she reached her stop. Fortunately the office rush precluded any sane conversation. She held on to Rohan's hand, almost dragging him to her door which she banged impatiently, glancing around over her shoulder, terror in her eyes.

"What's the hurry, I am coming," asked her mother as she opened the door.

Madhu burst in, took huge gulps of air and then burst into terrified sobs. All of them — Rohan, her mother, her sister-in-law Nita and brother Anil were bewildered. The latter glared at Rohan.

Rohan raised his shoulders and hands expressively.

"Don't ask me. Always thought Madhu to be extremely level headed, the way she has coped with her life. She looked a bit ill at the bus stop and asked me to bring her home. I thought you guys would know. But this...?" he gestured at the weeping woman with his hands, himself overcome at the total collapse of a colleague whose horrific story he knew and had admired her fight back.

Nita brought a glass of water and laid her arm around

Madhu's shoulders, "Here, drink this water and tell us what happened to you, Madhu."

As the cold water sank into the pit of her stomach, Madhu calmed enough to speak up:

"There's this guy out there. He's been following me for days..."

"Who? Where?" Anil threw the door open to look out but saw nothing.

Slowly the whole story came out — the unease, the prickly sensation as if she was being followed, Shirley's observation and her own in the past few days, and finally "Who could it be?"

The question hung in the air.

Day Six

Madhu stayed home the next day; Ma kept peeking out from behind the curtains of different windows to see if anyone was watching the house, but didn't see a soul. She was relieved.

Day Seven

The next day when Madhu reported seeing the hat and coat, Anil decided to call in reinforcements. He called a friend who knew someone at the local police station.

They waited for her at the home stop. Three pairs of eyes watched her alight from the bus, glance around apprehensively before heading home.

As she stopped to pick up her repaired chappal from the *mochi*, she swung around – but not quickly enough. But even as he ducked out of her vision, her predator was spotted.

Madhu headed home, checked at the doorstep to look back and spotted the hat and coat. Holding the door open, her mother pulled her in quickly. In the headlong rush to get in, Madhu missed the drama at the gate where Anil and a plainclothes man jumped on the guy to bundle him into a waiting jeep. Inside, they peeled off the disguise.

"You!" burst out Anil. "When did you get out of jail?" He lunged for the stalker and the policemen had to restrain him.

"What was he in jail for?" they asked Anil.

"Attempted murder and bride burning," Anil spat out.

The stalker was marched firmly into a cell as soon as they touched base. Meanwhile Anil had called his lawyer and waited for him to arrive before meeting the station head to explain his case. The station head understood.

During preliminary interrogation, the stalker stuck to one line:

"I never touched her. She is my wife. I want her back."

Finally a senior officer was called in.

"Why were you stalking that woman?"

"She's my wife. I want her back."

"You tried to kill her."

"That's a lie. I saved her life."

"The record shows a life sentence after you pleaded guilty."

"My lawyer told me to. It was to save my parents."

"Why?"

"I had to save my parents."

"Didn't they help you to set your wife on fire?"

"I could not let them go to jail."

"So you pleaded guilty?"

"Yes. Now I'm out. I want my wife back."

"Why should she come with you? You tried to murder her. Which sane woman would want to live with her murderer?"

"I didn't kill her. Actually after they set her on fire, I tried to save her. See, I have burn marks on my hands."

"Have you any idea of the burns she has had to contend with?"

"Nonsense. I put out the fire immediately with a blanket and rolling her on the floor."

During all this, Anil was being restrained to prevent him from butting in. The interrogator switched gears.

"You say you want your wife back. If she is your wife, why didn't you go and meet her and her family? Why stalk her like that? Were you hoping to frighten or kidnap her? Looks like that to me."

"You've got the wrong impression. I wanted to see her first. Also check out in case she had gotten married to someone else."

"And if she had?"

The stalker's face tightened. But he did not reply.

"What would you have done if she had remarried? Burnt her again, or killed her husband?"

"Do you think I am a professional butcher?"

"From what you did to her — Yes."

"What did I do to her? I saved her life when her sari was on fire."

"After selecting a synthetic sari to ensure maximum damage and asking for a cup of tea to send her into the kitchen, you set her on fire and closed the door. And then made a show of going in to help to save her life with a blanket?"

"Are you mad? Why would I burn her? She was my wife."

"Ok, I'll accept your view for a few minutes. She was your wife. Then why did your parents burn her? Did they not know you loved her?"

"She and Ma always had hassles over things."

"What hassles over what things?"

"She didn't bring anything with her. So we had to make everything for her. My parents were old and tired."

"So they decided that they would kill her and get you a brand new bride who would bring lots of things with her?"

"I don't understand your logic. I said I want my wife back and that I burnt my hands trying to save her life."

"Why did you let them burn her in the first place?"

"How could I stop them? My mother threatened to kill

herself otherwise."

"So you let them kill your wife?"

"I pushed them aside to save her…."

"After setting her aflame. Why did you do that?"

"I said I did not do that."

"Oh, yes, your parents did that. Why haven't you called them yet?"

"Leave them out of this."

"So you were planning to claim your wife and take her home again to them? To be set on fire again, because now her family has nothing to give after spending so much money on all those operations."

"What operations?"

"Didn't you know that she has had operations to rectify the damage that you did to her? Even her ears needed surgery because of those cheap metal earrings she wore."

"She looks fine."

"Perhaps she has more inner strength and better family values."

"You think I should have let my parents go to jail?"

It continued well past midnight. The officers signed out and told Anil to go home too. Jaws dropped at home when he told them the incredulous story: Sudhir, Madhu's husband was the stalker.

"How dared he? After trying to kill me? Will he be able to even look at all the scars, leave alone live with them?"

A video flashback shot before Madhu's eyes, finding herself enveloped in a burning sari, waking up in hospital, the endless treatments, operations, salves and oh-so-slow recovery; then the hunt for normalcy with a change of address and work with a changed persona, long hair and scarves covering her plastic surgery restored ears and long kurtas to cover the burnt areas of her torso until the grafts meshed. Before that she lived for almost three years in long gowns and never stepped out of the house, except to see doctors.

"Who said that he will look at or live with them? You think we will let you?"

Madhu looked up in surprise – Nita's voice rang out loud and clear.

"Madhu, enough. We are not going to repeat those mistakes," Nita said soberly. "When you used to come home and talk about being harassed for things, I didn't quite believe you. It was difficult to believe. Whatever you were given was just like what I'd got – my father gave the same to all my sisters as well. And no one complained. Even you never complained about my things.

"Why would anyone complain about your dowry? You were working too. Remember how much you used to make in tuitions? And," she went on shamefacedly, "along with disbelief was an element of selfishness. I was afraid you'd come back home and I wanted my own home. Perhaps that intensified my disbelief. But after what they did to you and your heroic fight back, I always felt terribly guilty that I might have been instrumental for your suffering at their hands. I'm sorry – forgive me." Nita held out her hands to Madhu, tears pouring down her cheeks.

The mother put a lid on any more soul searching with, "It is late now and tomorrow will be a very long day. All of you take sleeping pills and go to sleep. Now," she insisted.

In the morning, Anil spoke quietly, "Madhu, I'll try and avoid it if possible. But you may have to face Sudhir sometime. They haven't yet figured out his motives."

That remained a mystery. The stalker aka Sudhir did not call his parents to bail him out. Nor would he budge from his insistence that he wanted his wife back.

Anil's insides crunched every time Sudhir said that. He walked into the office of the station head:

"Sir, I need advice. That man was booked under Section 307 last time — attempt to murder and awarded a life sentence. How did he get out? What can I do to keep him out of my sister's life now?"

"A life sentence is usually 14 years, but some do get out earlier if they have behaved well in jail. He was smart enough to stay out of trouble somehow. Your second question had better be addressed to a lawyer."

In no time at all, the story hit the headlines; the first to descend on Madhu was obviously a team from the NGO she worked with; after all who else would give a job to a woman with such horrendous burn marks, except an organization working in the arena? Being professionals, they roped in the concerned officials from the family welfare and women's departments to meet the family.

A primary concern: "Why have you not taken a divorce in all these years, Madhu?" asked her boss, Ms. Somaiya.

Madhu gasped, stunned by that query.

"I — I never thought of it, Ma'am. And no one ever told me. Not even in the therapy I went through. Plus that medical circus and court case. My brother handled the court and I was in hospital. The medical issues continued with grafting on the torso burns and all that till I got totally fed up and decide to let it just be. I just stopped wearing saris and stuck to kurtas as cover-ups.

"My goal was to stand on my own feet. Even though we had shifted to a new locality, those fresh burn marks on my hands gave me away and no parents would send their kids for tuitions. That was when I reached you and opted for an inner office job, not to offend anyone's aesthetics. We – I never dreamt that even if he came out so soon, he would come chasing after me. What does he want? How can anyone be so shameless?"

"Madhu, you can be excused, but the rest of your family? They should have initiated divorce proceedings. Don't you know you can send the notice to the jail? In circumstances like this, there is usually little problem in securing a legal divorce; you would have been saved this entire trauma," explained Ms. Somaiya.

Nita spoke up, "Can any one of you tell us why he could possibly be demanding her back? It doesn't make sense after everything."

That question was the crux of the dilemma. Even the police had not been able to figure out Sudhir's intentions.

What they did agree to was that should he apply for bail, Madhu's lawyer would oppose unless he signed on the papers for a divorce on grounds of mutual consent – which would get through fastest.

But Mr Sudhir 'stalker' insisted that he wanted to talk to Madhu – to convince her to go back to him?

It took a lot of convincing for a Madhu, now terrified of being stalked, even when he was still in the lock up. Rather than an enraged Anil, it was Nita and Ms Somaiya who accompanied her to the police station, with guards on the ready. They did the talking, trying to get past the "She is my wife" stand.

"Why, after you have burnt her once?"

"I need her to look after my parents who are old and cannot manage on their own; I cannot manage both of them…" he mumbled, his head down.

Nita shot out: "Have you seen her?"

"Her face looks good," he averred.

"But the body? Her ears. What do you think...?"

"Let her talk," he cut Nita off. She had come prepared for just that. She spread a set of pictures on the table — of Madhu's burnt torso, ears and hands, taken before the start of treatment. Sudhir didn't react till he realized what it was and then gagged, trying not to throw up.

Madhu stood up. Leaning forward across the table, she spat in his face. "That is all I have to say to you," and walked out swiftly, leaving the others to follow.

Ms Somaiya preached caution and a nuanced approach.

"Madhu that does not solve this problem. He cannot be held indefinitely in the lock up. You will have to file a complaint and face him in court. To what end? How much punishment? Also divorce proceedings. How does his mind work? If he is vindictive, he can do much more harm. We have to protect her...." Her appeal was directed at the family.

"She has been very brave all this time. Now?"

"We'll send her abroad," offered the mother. "My brothers are in Canada."

"That will take some time," countered Anil. "If she goes off abroad before the divorce is finalized, it will be hanging over her head even there. If she can go to Canada, maybe so can he."

"Since he was in jail for attempted murder, does that not make him a history sheeter? Can he get a passport?"

"Or can we get a restraining order?"

"Shouldn't she learn some self defense, like karate or judo or something?"

Everyone had something to say; Madhu listened quietly. When it petered out, she spoke up:

"May I say something? I happen to know that his passport would have expired while he was in jail, around the same time as mine – we had them done together, remember? Unless he does some hanky panky, it could not have been renewed. I would love to go abroad, but wouldn't that be running away? Why should I be lonely abroad when I have done nothing wrong and can lead my life here? Yes, self-defense makes sense – I'll have to ask the doctor which form will be best with my weak back? I'll need to buy a stock of Pepper spray too. But first, I need that divorce – I don't want to hear him saying I am 'his' wife!

"Madam," Madhu turned to her NGO Head, "I need your help and support: a lawyer smart enough to keep him inside – on any grounds – until the divorce is through. Someone who can tell him that if he does not want the mutual consent route, then we'll file and I'll go on the stand to tell everything he and his parents did, with media coverage."

There was a collective gasp. Last time, with all that horrendous burn damage, she had refused to allow the media into her affairs. Now?

"I'll not cover up with kurtas but wear a sari," looking

at the astonished circle around her, Madhu's voice firmed, "which will show off the scars, highlighted with make-up to make them stand out more. Now that I have faced him once, I'll do it again and again in court. Look him straight in the eye and call him and his parents murderers when he says, 'take care of my parents.' Madam, we have media links – get them started on 'The Stalker' case, please. If we can drag his parents into court that will break him perhaps?"

When Madhu paused to catch her breath, Ms Somaiya spoke up, "Why the Stalker? Instead of giving him that publicity, why not 'The Stalked,' the woman with her chin up?"

A Mahabharatian Casting Couch

"Such a stupid woman. I won't have anything to do with her and you had better not also." The tone was emphatic, rather dictatorial.

"Do you know who she is?"

"What does that matter? She is a Bitch with a capital B."

"Don't be a fool. She is the Boss's wife."

"So? Because she is wife of your boss, she's right?"

"Right or wrong, just be polite; if you don't like her, maintain some reserve."

"Reserve my foot. If she talks nonsense, I'll tick her off."

"Then forget that foreign holiday. How do you think you'll get that without my being on the boss's right side?"

"Poor man's probably fed up of her too. I'll bet on it."

"He's fed up of everything. He likes smart women who

sleep all their way up."

"Oh yes, that's how men will always talk about women who are smarter than them," her voice dripped acid.

"Smita, listen, believe it or not, people do it to go up. Sometimes its physical, sometimes mental, sometimes both. Old men who are tired of the wives' demands and prefer brash, eager-to-please guys. Or sometimes to service their wives while they play elsewhere. Or just plain tired. It could even be a secretary or executive looking for a ride up. Who are we to judge anybody?"

"Not anybody. But you, yes. Tell me, how did you become Assistant Regional Manager?"

"Now that's asking Smita." She bridled at the smile on his face. Her face tightened as she demanded shrilly, "Her or him?"

"What'll you do, if I say both?" he teased gently. She lashed out with her hands, but he fended her off as he wrestled to keep the car on the road.

"Don't be a fool, Smita. The other day, you and your kitty friends were giggling about the exchange sandals and car keys games for couples, weren't you? Come on and admit it, were you not?"

"So what if we were gossiping?"

"There's no smoke without fire. If they can go off for a fling with the car key owner, just for the heck of it, why not with the Boss for the husband's promotion? How do you think your Pandu and Vidura and Dhritarashtra were born? By Ved Vyas looking into their mothers' eyes passionately? Are you such a fool?"

"Don't give me all that crap. I want to know about your promotion."

"You just want a story, don't you? Ok listen – we were two guys and two couples at a holiday resort. Incentive bonus with a bachelor boss. One wife was uptight… they got posted to Assam. Of the remaining three men, the one with the sexy-eyed wife became the Regional Manager and the other two A R Ms. What would you rather do, get f**ked or slide to the bottom? Remember the fates of those three guys?"

"Who?"

"Pandu, Vidura and Dhritarashtra. Their fates were sealed by how their mothers took it, wasn't it?"

Scot Free

"Why should he get off scot free? He wrecked my life, my little world. I don't want him back. I am happy as I am now. Free to lead my life as I want it, not as he or his relatives want me to lead it.

Neelima was smarting from a marriage gone awry late in the day. "During those slog overs, I supported Pankaj unstintingly. Now that the good days have come, he's upped and gone, leaving me high and dry, with a teenage brood to manage on my own," she wailed; then brooded: 'When did it all come to this?'

That year summer had an unusual flavour for underneath the dusty heat was a distinct chill. Usually, summer meant early mornings and late nights of cool, pleasant weather. But that year, it had been cool even in the day, with an underlying foreboding of chill. Was it a premonition of disaster, of some untoward event or what?

They'd celebrated his entry into TV, which meant much more money than theatre had ever given. It was too early for that foreign holiday yet, but a new home and car were on the cards and so were so many new goodies.

And all of a sudden, there was that ominous notice. And then…

The end of the marriage, after half-a-lifetime of being together.

Even months later, Neelima was still resentful.

"What actually do you want now?" asked her friend Priya gingerly.

"That he should be made a public example of. His family just accepted his verdict 'I want a divorce', without so much as asking what the problem was or attempting any sort of a reconciliation. Why didn't they?"

"Is that how you want your husband? Not out of love, or even concern for you and the kids; but tied to your apron strings, against his wishes, a prisoner of family pressures, the joint pressures of his parents, uncles and aunts, brothers and sisters."

That was tragic but true. Neither of their families had attempted to bring about a reconciliation. Letting a twenty year old marriage go down the drain, for want of an effort? And in the case of the two concerned parties, for want of a lowering of the ego?

"Heaven help you! How long do you think such a union will last? Realistically speaking, if the wedges come in young age and family pressures combine to hold a marriage together for some time, it may survive due to sheer inertia or development of habits.

"But so late in life? When a man is a well-developed personality in his own right, is no longer dependent or swayed by emotional blackmail of the familial kind, if he decides to go — go he will and not all the acid-tongued aunts in the world can prevent him. If you continue to rave and rant, you will only show the world why he decided to call it a day and the sympathy balance will tilt in his favour, not yours."

"What about me, my needs, my desires? My pride? Don't they count at all?"

Her friend looked away unhappily. What balm could she offer the troubled soul? How difficult it was to confront an unhappy person with realities of her own actions and say, 'Look at it from his point of view.'

Priya and her husband had just come away from meeting the estranged husband, full of his woes recently multiplied after a property battle with Neelima's successor, his new wife Vidya.

"It's the cleft stick. For once it will not be the woman who'll take the blame for the break-up of the marriage. I'll have to shoulder all the blame if Vidya walks out on me."

"What are you talking about?"

They were sitting on a meticulous lawn, overshadowed by the unwinking wooden elf — a tribal artefact picked up by Pankaj and tucked into a tiny artificial grove which Neelima had often fantasized about.

'So many people are jealous of this garden and he always stares at me so, as if wishing me dead,' she used to insist balefully.

"The tables have turned," said Pankaj. "Usually, no matter what, it is the lady who takes the blame for the break-up of the marriage. Everyone tells her that she should have learnt to adjust. But with Vidya, the odds are stacked against me."

"How?"

"She has given me an ultimatum: either she gets control of all the property or she leaves."

"Then let her leave. You don't need that quarrelsome bitch. Get another."

Priya gave her husband a malevolent look. 'How dare you?' it said.

"Are you mad? At this age? Can't you just hear them?"

'That old scaly bastard. First he slept around. When he was caught red-handed, he ditched his wife on the eve of their silver wedding anniversary to marry another woman. Now even that new one wants out.' At a time when people plan their children's marriages, I will face a second divorce!

"Everyone, but everyone asked me, 'why now?' More than half of life is gone already. Have you any idea of the number of times I asked myself the same question before the split with Neelima? Why now? When I stood her for so long, why now? What difference will it make? If I could make it in spite of Neelima, instead of because of her support, why uproot my life after making it.

"But it does make a difference, a big difference. Peace and quiet, no quarrels or abuses, a civilized life concentrating on the fine points of my craft, entertaining friends, being entertained in a civilized, cultured manner.

"The downside is that I lost my family, my children. Yes, there are children in the family, my sister's, brother's, nephew. Not mine. I miss them — their grumbling, their complaining and their little jokes. Initially I was angry. My ego hurt that my children preferred their mother over me, despite having been witness to her irrational behaviour over the years, her neglect of them and the home. Her rabid insistence on curfews.

"It was crazy. When my son was 16 and ripe for a 10 o'clock curfew, she insisted on eight o'clock. What full blooded teenager will accept that when the evening only began at seven? Incessant battles and me as arbitrator? Yet, they stayed put and I let them be, for her to lean on. But Neelima sent them away. She does not need anything, except her ego. Now I have to deal with Vidya, who does not need anything but her name on some of the solid family real estate, so that she is never 'left high and dry'? Not that I left Neelima high and dry, but the fear seems to have made a greater home in Vidya's heart.

"Did Neelima actually say that I was getting off scot free?"

Akhri Kshun: The Last Moments

Juhi was livid.

The massive TV showed a stylish Layla by Sachin's bed at the hospital. She had appeared out of nowhere after Sachin's illness was made public; reaching the hospital with the media and OB vans in tow, she put her arms around the white-haired and obviously weak Sachin to place a kiss on his forehead.

"Who does she think she is? Landing from the US to meet her long lost husband, with OB vans in tow? Look at them billing and cooing. Had she informed the press in advance for publicity? As if everyone doesn't know that the media will do anything for a story!"

The family drama being played out on TV was 'Oh so touching!' Sachin and Layla sat holding hands, gazing into each other's eyes and shedding a few tears. Layla brought forward their two girls and Sachin wept on seeing them.

Picking up her mobile, Juhi called her party secretary. A rapid fire conversation followed and in no time at all, chaos erupted on the TV screen. "*Hai hai* Layla", "Go back Layla" rent the air as party workers screamed venom for the cameras. It was full-scale politics.

Inside, the hospital authorities called on Layla. Herself a media veteran, she understood the exigencies all too well and quietly agreed to a backdoor exit.

"There is nothing much that can be done for him here which cannot be done at home by nursing aides. It would be better that neither he nor other patients are disturbed by unruly elements," the hospital superintendent reasoned with Juhi, requesting her to take Sachin home to allow the hospital to function in peace for its other non-celebrity patients.

Shortly after the OB vans left, an ambulance brought Sachin home. But not to peace. Heckles raised, Layla did not sit quiet. The evening news telecast interviews with her erstwhile colleagues.

"We remain married — yes — still. We have two daughters and that is an unbreakable bond between us, even though we have lived apart for decades now. When I heard that he was at the terminal stage of cancer, I had to come. His daughters had to meet him too."

"Why? Why did you live apart if you did not wish to

break that bond?"

"Every person evolves. Maybe our evolution took place in different directions, therefore the break. But can anyone wish ill to the father of one's children?"

Cameras whirred while stations replayed the morning telecast of the couple embracing in hospital. Ammaji was all eyes; she wiped away her own tears, quite impervious to Juhi's ranting, which grew worse as she let fly at Sachin's mother.

"Why do I have to watch your tears now? Sitting here all day with that mournful face, making others want to cry too. This is no way to show sympathy. Your son is not dead yet; but if he sees you weeping all day, he'll probably die tomorrow. Why don't you go home, meet your friends, play cards, sing bhajans or something? Anything but showing me that tear-stained face — please."

As she spoke, Juhi's volume rose steadily and the nurse appeared with a stern, "Volume down please. We can hear you inside too and Sachin Sir is awake."

For her part, Ammaji could just stare blankly at Juhi's face. Suddenly she stood up and walked out of the door, looking straight ahead, almost unseeing. She crossed the lane without taking in the waves of the neighbours or the smiles of passers-by. Reaching her home, she pushed the gate open and sat down heavily in the tiny verandah for quite a while before visibly collecting herself.

Ammaji let herself in; switched on the TV, then switched

it off again as the replays of Layla's interviews appeared. She switched on the radio and then immediately switched it off. She looked around her living room until her eyes fell on a stack of diaries on the bookshelf. Carefully, she picked them up and placed them on her little dining table. In her kitchen, she made herself a cup of coffee and brought it to the table with some biscuits in a tin, munching slowly as she leafed through her diaries.

Sachin's birth, his growing up, school, college, and the day he brought Layla home for the first time.

"She's Muslim?"

"So what? Isn't she human?"

"What will your father say?"

"Has he ever said anything except 'No'? In any case, he's not here anymore. He's so busy with his new woman; where does he have time for us?"

"Whatever the case, he is your father. You will have to take his permission."

"The hell with his permission. Tell me, do you like her?"

"She seems alright with you. Who are her parents?"

"How does that matter?"

"Then how do I matter?" replied Ammaji tightly. The debate continued into the night. Two days later, Sachin brought Layla again, this time both wore garlands and she had *sindoor* in her parting.

"It was a court marriage," he announced.

Layla fitted into their household well enough. Her mother was a well-known journalist, widowed young enough to make her daughter a very independent person. Both Sachin and Layla were prominent in socialist and media circles, busy with their respective careers while Ammaji was busy raising their girls. But not so busy that she did not see their lives diverging.

Sachin was changing ever so imperceptibly, especially in the eyes which had loved him too long. Power is an intoxicant. Compromises became the order of the day, the hell with ideology. Money was the name of the game.

As the girls grew up, Sachin's changed ideologies became more evident, especially to his friends. It troubled Layla. One night he dashed in late and demanded:

"Give me all the money in the house."

"When has there been much money in this house?"

"Shut up, the police is on its way." He dumped a couple of changes in a cloth bag, grabbed her chain and bangles and rushed off with a couple of hundred rupee notes. A nervous Layla called her mother, who arrived to carry off Ammaji, the girls and Layla to her own home.

Mother and daughter argued late into the night. Finally, she called in Ammaji and said,

"Ammaji, talk to her. Emergency is being declared and Sachin is on the wrong side of the fence. Today I can get Layla a good job in the US; maybe not tomorrow; will socialism feed and educate these girls?"

Within a week, with a lot of string pulling, Layla was winging away to the West, Ammaji and the girls ensconced in her mother's home till she could afford to fetch them. That did not take too long with her UN media job. Only Ammaji refused to go.

"I am happy here; we two old women will keep each other company. All that change will be too much for me to cope with," she demurred.

Sachin was on another trip altogether. He had his high-flying friends and a very special friend, Juhi, who funded his business ventures as regularly as they flopped around his ears. Juhi was a classic parlour-boutique polished heiress, vacillating between politics and entrepreneurship with total abandon. He was totally unashamed of admitting, "I live on Juhi's money until she funds my next venture."

Which was why, when he offered a home to Ammaji, she demurred.

Layla's mother had just passed away and he appeared out of the blue, declaring, "Come with me now. Why live with strangers?"

"*Beta,* this is not a stranger's home. It now belongs to Layla."

"Where is she? She hasn't remembered me in all these years."

"Have you? Even your girls?"

"Let's forget the past. At least come and see my home."

Lonely and bereft, Ammaji caved in. It did not take her long to assess Juhi and her daughter Monica, for whom 'smoking like chimneys and drinking like fish' was a way of life.

Layla wrote: "Ammaji, we'll sell Ma's house. Look out for a smaller place close to Sachin so that you can be close and yet have your own roof and privacy and the girls can come to visit you, without getting in the way of Those Two."

Of course, Juhi was furious. "Why two establishments to add to living expenses?"

Ammaji flashed, "Don't worry, Juhi; I have enough money of my own. And if ever I need more, I can always call Layla." She said it deliberately, knowing it would infuriate Juhi who loved the 'rich woman supporting all relatives' act. In vain did Sachin argue but Ammaji was adamant.

She found herself a little house; Layla flew down for the elaborate formalities of sale and purchase of houses, placed the money in Ammaji's account and flew back after making friends with the neighbours to request:

"Please keep an eye on my mother and give me a call whenever the need arises."

When eyebrows were raised over this request, she elaborated, "My husband, her son will be useless in a crisis."

Walls have ears and ears have feet. When that remark reached Juhi, with a lot of added masala, her giant tantrum ensured that Sachin did not even meet Ammaji for almost six months.

Ammaji continued leafing through her diaries. Now Sachin began to leave business decisions to Juhi and turned to the wheeling and dealing in government circles for the business deals that gave a leg up to Juhi's parties. She was to be interviewed and needed a 'happy family' image.

Sachin and Juhi turned up at Ammaji's house, touching her feet and begging forgiveness with crocodile tears. Poor Ammaji; she was all alone, Layla was far away and Sachin was here at her feet, begging for forgiveness, begging her to come to his home at least once.

What could an old woman do? Ammaji went.

When the press photographer entered and Monica slid into place on the arm of her chair, she felt totally manipulated; but it was too late and she smiled graciously into the camera. But, as soon as they left she was very firm.

"Now I must go to my home. My peace is as precious to me as your privacy is to you people. Whenever you wish, do come and see me. Perhaps we can all have lunch together on Sundays…if you wish…."

Ammaji was absolutely firm on her decision; secretly Juhi and her daughter Monica were thrilled. But the scandal! The gossip it generated! Especially when Ammaji made regular trips to the US and stayed with Layla for weeks, but never spent a night under Sachin's roof. Sachin came once a week to meet her, his women infrequently.

Ammaji picked up a pen and began to write:

'It was only Sachin's illness which compelled me to spend time under his roof again. If only I had restrained myself, Juhi would not have had a chance to....

Unable to frame the rest of the sentence, Ammaji wearily put her head down to rest on the table and passed out — and passed on forever.

In the morning, nobody answered the milkman's bell. Her mobile too remained unanswered. After sometime, the maid came. When there was no reply, she left happily pausing to chat with the security guard.

"Maybe Ammaji is at her son's since he is ill. If you meet her, tell her I am going to the village for at least three days. Since she will there all the time, she won't really need me, I think."

No-one thought much more of it, not even the milkman. Everyone assumed Ammaji must be with her son. When the maid came back, she rang the bell and sensed something strange around, something almost malodorous. She called out to a neighbour: "Have you seen Ammaji?"

"She must be at Sachinji's."

The next day the maid went along to Sachin's place but Juhi was nonchalant.

"I am busy with his illness. She is just throwing a tantrum and I have no intention of going to touch her feet. If she doesn't want to see her sick son, what can I do?"

The maid was stunned.

"But Ammaji is not at home. The milkman, security guard and neighbours all said so."

"Don't nag here. Please go. She must have gone to Layla." The next day when the maid turned up, there was a small crowd of neighbours at Ammaji's door. The smell was even more powerful; and since Ammaji's whereabouts were not known, the police had been called. A self important sub-inspector put in a belated appearance.

"We'll need to break open the door," he explained.

"Her son lives close-by."

"Why didn't you say so first? Let's call him."

Juhi appeared demanding angrily, "Why have you called us? Don't you know Sachin is serious?"

The sub-inspector intervened, explaining that the door would have to be broken open and that a family member was necessary to avoid later complaints of thefts and break-ins. But as soon as the door opened, the smell sent several women vomiting in the shrubs. The inspector and his men tied handkerchiefs over their faces to enter.

Ammaji was slumped over her table. Her hand clutched her pen on the open page of the diary which revealed her last thoughts.

The inspector was smart enough to take charge of the diary and call his senior before sending off the body. Since

Juhi had kept her distance, she did not know that. The police landed at her doorstep and marched in. Juhi's voice was loud and piercing. The nurse came out to tap her on the shoulder:

"Madame, Sir is asking what has happened?"

"Nothing that concerns him."

The nurse backed away. But curious as the proverbial cat, she left the door ajar to hear what was going on outside with the police and their questions.

"Madam, we are not taking you to the station because of your husband's condition. So please co-operate and answer properly. When did you last see Ammaji?"

"Must have been three or four days ago. Who knows? We have been so busy we don't keep track of time or days. You know, the doctors have told us there is no hope for Sachin so we have just to take one day at a time. Now this?"

"What happened the last time Ammaji came here?"

"Nothing."

"Something must have happened. That interview on TV?"

"That is our personal family matter."

A mobile buzzed inside. The nurse answered and then handed it over to Sachin, "Layla Madam."

"But did you not wonder why a mother would not come to look up her so sick son for four-five days?"

"Who has the time for all that? I'm busy and besides, she was almost senile."

The constable came in to whisper in his senior's ear.

"Madam, the neighbours say that you fought with her."

"Who bothers about gossip?" Juhi's voice started its upward trail again.

"The last entry in the diary says that you did something...."

"Nonsense."

"The handwriting in the diary has matched that in the older ones. It is hers."

Juhi let out a string of vile curses, so loud, the Inspector was as shocked as the curious neighbours crowding around the windows and verandah.

The nurse turned around to glance at her charge. He was sitting up and gasping for breath. The mobile had fallen from his grasp and he was reaching for it. Before she could reach him, he gave a huge sigh and breathed his last.

The nurse closed his open eyes and covered his face with the sheet, wondering —

'Had he heard Juhi in his last moments? Did he know why, despite his terminal cancer, his mother had preceded him in death?'

Salaam Memsahib

Papaji looked happily at his little family.

With God's Grace, things had turned out well and the turmoil of his twenties had settled down quite satisfactorily.

'How much was it thanks to his phlegmatic wife and her powers of organization?' he often wondered.

He took in his wife, now well past her prime, filling out as she had never dared to in her youth and bent double with pain, but greying quite handsomely nevertheless. She had set the example for her daughters, in the true Punjabi Never-Say-Die spirit, carrying on blithely with a brave face for the world to see, red lipstick always intact.

Now in a few days time, both grandsons would be getting married and starting lives of their own. He glanced proudly at his two daughters, so very alike, almost twins, he thought fondly.

Both Ranjana and Sonali were tall, handsome women in their prime, just two years apart. They had been put through identical paces, he recalled, by their mother; they had been to the same nursery classes, then the same convent school, learnt identical lessons from their mother, sitting with a little bamboo in her hand. Together they had mastered the intricacies of stitching, knitting reams of shawls and sweaters and even making pickles. And although they had married a year apart, they had had their boys together, virtually days apart.

Neither had gone in for a second try, on the off chance of producing a daughter. 'Remain in the plus', their mother had advised and they had heeded.

Both sons-in-law were Services men, one Air Force and the other Army. No doubt one had opted for premature retirement earlier on, but with the other one now approaching retirement, the odds had levelled once again.

Even their houses were quite similar. Like all Services homes across the country, whether lodged in ultra-modern flats or older bungalow-style accommodations, the flavour was typical: greenery in pots at the entrance with a little cloth doll holding chits for callers to leave signatorial evidence of their visit, furniture interspersed with packing-box seaters, the almost mandatory painting / batik / embroidery by the lady wife, the shining brassware, the collection of mementoes from each station served, and either driftwood to indicate a sea-shore posting or woven pictures signifying a sojourn in Bhutan or the Northeast.

The elder Ranjana was statuesque, tall, shapely, and extremely well-preserved. Frequent parlour visits had given her that typical steamed cabbage complexion which was set off by perfectly styled hair and immaculate manicures.

She was a proper Services wife, running a disciplined house, managing the Women's Welfare and assorted committees with practised ease, setting an exacting example for the Station's younger wives.

On the other hand, Sonali's twitter dominated her personality and her social life, or so the fond father thought.

Ranjana tended to favour greys, greens or a black and white combination, with spectacular accessories and an air of sophistication which contrasted with the gaudy crimsons, loud pinks and cheeky oranges which Sonali flaunted with her easy-care hair style and no-nonsense make-up, with little time to spare for any accessory matching, except lots of gold.

What Papaji did not know, did not disturb him: that the major difference in the two otherwise identical-on-the-surface-households, with their typically Services flavour, was the sexual regime.

His elder daughter, Ranjana, had imposed a strict *Budh-Shani* (Wednesday-Saturday) regime on her husband, diverting his energies up the promotion ladder to land him early honours. The younger one, Sonali, was very much putty in her husband's hands, or rather demands; her giggling laughter was silenced only twice a day, noon and night, without which he was very, very irritable.

That night, Papaji expounded on his 'identical twins' theme to his wife, who replied tautly:

"God made each of our five fingers different. So how can two sisters be identical? Don't talk rubbish. They are not even twins. Actually there is a world of difference between the two; maybe you have not observed closely enough."

He had argued vociferously against that edict. "Why," he demanded, "why are you trying to create differences where there aren't any? What is the difference between Ranju's dominating, sometimes even cold nature and Sonali's chirpy giggling? Both are equally sharp and worldly-wise; could they have been otherwise, being your daughters?" he made a quick dig.

Beeji decided it was now time to open his eyes.

"So girls, how far have the preparations progressed? All the gifts etc., ready, anything still to be procured or packed?"

"What gifts are you talking about? Since when did we accept dowry?" growled the old man.

Ranjana moved to soothe his ruffled feathers immediately. "Even when there is no dowry etc., one has a lot to do in a marriage. And this is a double one, so that much extra organization for the guests; Who will sleep where? provisioning, menus and all that. Rahul will be leaving for his honeymoon immediately, but it will only be a very short one, so I'll also be leaving immediately for Jodhpur...."

"When did your Jodhpur posting come?"

"Not mine, Rahul's. Now he's getting married, we've managed to organize accommodation for them. So I'll be going to set it up before they arrive, as they'll not have time to come to our house in Delhi before he has to report. Besides, a bride should not arrive to unopened boxes, should she? What does a civilian bride know about uniform kits and service kitchens in balconies? I'll just settle them in and leave the next day. Later, they'll come to us for a longer visit."

"What about her things, her trousseau, jewellery, sofa set, bed and things?" queried Sonali.

"What things? We had said nothing except her personal belongings, which will be with her. Where are they going to cart around sofa sets and beds on various postings? They'll be using issue furniture for at least a decade, if not more. I'll organize that along with the kitchen when I reach there. Don't tell me you have asked for all that stuff?"

"All we said was that traditions must be followed...."

"But," interrupted Ranjana, "traditions are what we make of them. It could be a pillow and bedspread, or a blanket, or a fifty-thousand worth Kashmiri carved bed."

"Nothing of that sort. We promised Sanjay that we would not ask for anything and we have not. When they came to visit us, we took them over to our new farmhouse, which is under construction and showed them around. They saw everything for themselves, what all is there and what still needs to be provided. Naturally after the wedding..." She prattled on with further details of the glamorous accessories still to be installed, consciously innocuous, perhaps deliberately ignorant of the sharp looks on her sister's and father's faces and the bemused knowing one on her mother's.

Papaji looked into his wife's eyes and saluted.

Salaam Memsahib.

White Saris: Widow's Garb

"*Sasuma* (mother-in-law), I thought you may not have any, so I brought plain white saris for you."

The brand-new folded white saris sat almost innocently on his outstretched hands. A casual onlooker would have easily mistaken the gesture for one of filial concern. But the look in her son-in-law's eyes was anything but filial concern. Sinister triumph chased a sardonic question in his intense look at her.

She suspected, that much as he admired it, her son-in-law had always resented her easy elegance, the colourful saris and the restrained dignity of a single piece of jewellery, which contrasted with his ill-dressed mother and her particularly drab wardrobe. His eyes asked a question.

'Now what are you going to do, without your Lion to

protect you?'

She recognized the question, but her mind refused to grope for the answer. The woman was struggling yet with her own intense emotions at her husband's death. Silent tears poured unchecked down her cheeks, as eyes and brain grappled with the knowledge, 'He's dead? Dead?'

She was out on a routine trip — covering far flung villages on her way up the Ghats, meetings in Mumbai and on the way back, a stopover at an old aunt's at Karjat for a brief catching up with the family gossip.

The call caught up with her as she set out from Karjat 'Come home quickly.' But the usual Ghat jams had delayed her and she arrived too late. Instead of holding his hands at the end, she was left staring at the lifeless visage that had dominated her life for over a quarter of a century.

The children were all there. And the grandchildren. They had been with him at the end.

"At least he was not alone," intoned someone unctuously — almost accusingly.

There was no need for it. For Pushpa was only too conscious that despite the presence of the children and their children, her husband must have felt lonely without her.

"What happened?" finally she pushed the words out of tight lips turned to stone.

"Nothing. He was just sitting out watching the children play. Just before lunch Jatinbabu's car turned into the gate and Chhotu just missed crashing into it as he chased his ball. Sahib got up and started shouting, as he usual does, then he started to cough and sweat and then he fell down. We brought him in and called the doctor and Chhota Sahib…" the manservant's voice trailed off. "What could I do, memsahib, you were not there…."

Another guilt trip? Did anyone know he would collapse like this? He was hale and hearty when he saw her off this morning?

"Sasuma, I have brought these plain white saris for you. You'll need them now."

The words impinged into Pushpa's wandering thoughts. She blinked and focused on the sardonic smile on her son-in-law's face, as he proffered the white saris.

He was always a stickler for the niceties that kept women pinned down in mundane details unable to see the larger pictures of life.

'Why is he making such an issue of white saris?' thought her blanked-out mind. Immediately another thought chased the question, "I am a widow now. And white saris are for widows."

But even as her mind spoke the words, it did not will her hands to reach out to accept the proffered plain white saris. Mother-in-law and son-in-law faced each other for a seeming eternity, neither actually seeing nor recognizing the feelings of the other, until he spoke again.

"Don't worry. You can pay me for them later. At least wear one now. People will be coming soon." He knew he had never been allowed to spend a penny.

Even as a spark of anger started to flare in the woman's eyes, a calm hand stayed her response.

"Come Ma, you don't need these just now. You can wear one of your old ones." Her son took her firmly by the shoulders and led her into her bedroom. They stopped in the doorway, as she took in the familiar tranquility of her cool room, the worn drapes, the pictures on the walls, the comfortable old-fashioned chairs, everything was the same, familiar — but suddenly so empty. So bereft of the booming voice that never let anyone rest.

Abruptly the steel seemed to slither out of her spine. Pushpa almost collapsed as she bent her head to rest it on her son's shoulder.

Then as the tears again seeped through the closed eyelids, she spoke brokenly, "I am so tired of standing straight. Let me lean on you for some time. All his life, he leaned on me. All the time, every time. Sometimes lightly, sometimes heavily, but always he leaned. I could never relax under that weight and I am so tired of standing straight."

Her son put both his strong arms protectively around his murmuring mother. He let her weep, conscious of the watchful eyes of his brother-in-law leaning forward to eavesdrop.

Finally the mother whispered, "Let me lie down. I can't stand anymore."

Gently he led her to the bed. "Cover me," she said and he tucked the coverlet around her. She caught his hand. "Sit with me for a bit," she pleaded.

He heard a gurgle behind him from his brother-in-law, as he bent over to knead his mother's tense back and shoulders into relaxation.

A whirlwind blew in. "Bhaiya, oh good, let Ma rest a bit. She'll need all her strength later. And what are you doing here? And what is this? Who brought these shiny white saris? Don't you know that one doesn't wear this new shiny stuff at a time like this? Ridiculous nonsense. I'll give them to the servants to at least wash and iron them to get the shine and the starch out…"

As she plucked the saris out of her husband's hands and whirled off, she also took the look of scheming violence from his eyes.

The old Lion was gone but the young cubs were his offspring alright. They wouldn't let anyone maul the Lion's Mate.

Hell Hath No Fury As A Woman Spurned

'The author's insipid language wastes the themes and insults the emotions of the characters, assaulting the intelligence of the readers…' wrote the critic.

"Who the hell is this? How dare she write such rubbish in a literary review? Ma, you must respond."

"Literary critics have the freedom to praise or criticize. She is doing her job, as she sees fit."

"It has to be more than that. Why is only her opinion different? Everyone else has given favourable reviews."

"Then she's different."

"Ma, this is a personal attack. You know each other. Confront her at the reading," insisted Ria.

"I'll do no such thing. Saraiya is exercising her right to her opinion. Any public brouhaha may lose me my positive reviews. Also bring charges of raking up a controversy as a marketing tactic."

"That's a wonderful idea. If this one sells well, they'll really flock back. We all want this book to sell. If a debate can generate sales, why not?"

"What is there to debate?" remonstrated the mother.

"This lousy personal attack. There has to be a reason behind it. A critic can't write anything because she happened to be in a foul mood or had a fight just before she wrote it."

"Maybe the story touched a raw nerve, some personal experience? Ma, how well do you know Saraiya? Do we know anyone who knows her, so we can get in touch and find out? We'll ferret out her skeletons to expose her."

"Stop that. All of you. I know Saraiya. Maybe not too well, but enough, okay."

"So?"

"So nothing. I know why she has trashed my work. It is nothing but delayed vengeance."

"Vengeance? Against whom?"

"Drop it. I don't want to debate this. If my book doesn't sell because of this review, I have a family, my husband and children to help me over the disappointment. She is all alone — no husband, no children and is passing through relationships. The public scandal will break her."

"What scandal? That she brought her personal life into her professional one?"

Nandita walked into the refuge of her study. 'Saraiya,' she thought, 'what have you done?' It was difficult to even conjure up the face to match the name.

Her husband Alok walked in. "Tell me, what is this all about?"

"It happened so long ago I'd almost forgotten the incident. Saraiya seems to have stoked the hurt and bided her time to wreck vengeance for a totally unwitting act on my part." Nandita stopped to collect her memories as she gazed out of the window.

"It happened ages back at a college festival. From the magazines, I gather Saraiya has become refined. She used to be very outspoken and dominating, almost aggressive; her hair was cropped boyishly; she wore pants and pathani suits, never salwar-kurtas.

"Today she occasionally chooses to dazzle Page 3 with a stunning outfit; but never a sari in public. That is only for her grandmother's pujas."

Oblivious of the growing number of listeners, Nandita delved into her memory. "Ever since I've known her, Saraiya walked like a man, ordering everyone about, talking down to women like men. Only that dulcet voice was a total mismatch coming out of that shirt-collared throat. She really had to practice hoarse speaking for her male roles in college plays. She sings beautifully, but she hated the gentle songs that suited her voice, preferring to belt out raunchy numbers that sounded really naughty in her voice.

"Despite those naughty songs, I never suspected anything. I did not realize what she had wanted of me until a few years back. Naive fool that I was, I hadn't comprehended what she wanted and spurned her totally uncomprehendingly. She must have been quite hurt, I presume. That is why this delayed vengeance. She never got a chance earlier."

"Ma, what vengeance, what hurt? You are talking in riddles."

Nandita swung around to find her family gathered behind her. Her husband was flanked by her two married daughters and son. "When did you come?"

"Long ago; doesn't matter. What did you do?"

A rueful smile played on Nandita's lips.

"Come on, Ma, now we've heard the prelude, you have to tell us the rest. What did you do?"

"Nothing."

"Ma...."

"Honestly, that's the problem. I did nothing then and I'm paying for it now. And will continue to do nothing because if I speak out now, it will sound like a revengeful reply to her criticism."

"Pa, do something. Ma's talking in riddles."

The old couple exchanged a long look and comprehension gleamed in the old man's eyes. "Uh-huh?"

His wife nodded slowly. "I took much longer to

understand", she said, deep regret in her voice. "What could I do?" A degree of asperity crept into her voice. "Enough, an old woman is entitled to her own secrets." she told her children.

"No," said Ria flatly. "In a family, no secrets. You taught us that Ma. Now you want to hold out on us? Now, when everyone is pointing fingers and asking questions?"

Then she resumed more quietly.

"Ma, trust us. We will not unnecessarily publicize unpleasantness. But we need to understand what this is all about. Have some faith in the training that you have given us all these years."

The older couple exchanged another look, smiles lifting the corners of their mouth unwittingly. She had struck the nail on the head.

"Listen, Saraiya and I met at a college festival play. I was in-charge of the costumes." Nandita paused, gathering her memories. "She kept putting off trying on her costume. Thinking she felt shy, I took the costume to her room. She was alone and asked me to latch the door. 'Come on, we're all the same,' I ribbed her. When I turned around, there was Saraiya, stark nude, standing on her clothes." There was a muted gasp from Nandita's little audience. She had no underclothes. Can you imagine how embarrassed I was? I didn't know where to look! She had a shapely figure inside those baggy pathanis, perfectly shaped small breasts, a narrow waist flowing gracefully into wide hips, long legs. She held out her hands, and I...."

"What did you do Ma?" The worldly-wise daughters' question was almost impatient.

"I pulled the costume over her head to cover her nakedness and to see if it fitted."

"Aw...w...w, come on Ma..."

"That is the whole problem. I was so naive, I didn't know what the gesture meant. Even had I known, how would I have handled that?" the old woman asked herself.

"I merely took it as a part of Saraiya's extravagant exhibitionism, brusquely fitted the costume and then carried it out. Actually I was so stunned, I couldn't meet her eyes. I didn't look at her properly at all. Maybe, if I had, I may have acted differently. She must have felt so totally rejected and humiliated, because upto that point, we had vibed quite well together."

"Then?"

"Then what? Nothing. I must have carried on, whatever, I don't remember. Saraiya was distant. You know me. I'm not too comfortable with exhibitionists. I decided that Saraiya was nothing but a shameless exhibitionist. For the life of me, I couldn't figure out what she had wanted to expose for me for?

"That came many years later. In between, we lost touch, before her marriage and its rapid break-up over her 'close friend' Shreela. People talked about their being always together and why Shreela never married. Sometimes, perhaps after a tiff, Saraiya would surface for a spell with some handsome hunk, but never marry him. She became more and more blunt and manly and I guess, guys felt safer with her than with simpering socialites whose marital claws may or not have been cleverly disguised.

"Only very recently did lightening strike. I finally realized what Saraiya had wanted of me that afternoon. But, so much water had flowed under the bridge, what was the point of raking it up with her or with anybody. I put it down to my inexperience and hoped that she may have done the same, although she must have been terribly hurt. That she would nurse such a grudge and wreck vengeance in this fashion. That ? That I would never ever have dreamt of."

Nandita shrugged her shoulders helplessly and put out her hands to her children, appealing for their understanding.

The elder Ria asked: "Is she coming for the launch tomorrow?"

"Lord knows," replied Nandita, a question mark on her face.

There was concern in his voice when her husband asked, "Nandu, what will you do if she does?"

Nandita looked into his eyes, her face pleading.

At the launch, Nandita was surrounded by friends and well wishers; but she was ill-at-ease and kept looking all around and over her shoulder as she signed books and responded to good wishes.

Saraiya swept in, clad in her Pathani suit and a snazzy jacket, accompanied by Shreela who had spent a couple of hours persuading her to put the past behind; and to show that by attending the launch. Many rushed forward to wish her.

Shreela was talking to an acquaintance when she looked around and spotted Saraiya – face to face with Nandita.

Saraiya's congratulations were a bit stilted; but Nandita's smiled 'thanks' was genuine enough. But before the ice could be properly broken, her daughter came up to hand a mobile to Nandita; she had perforce to excuse herself as she moved away.

Ria was on hospitality duty. "Have you had some coffee?"

"Thanks, but no thanks," Saraiya replied stiffly.

"Are you Ma's friend?" asked Ria curiously.

"Old college friends. I am Saraiya."

Rai froze, pulled a long face and started to walk off as Nandita came back.

Saraiya's face was a question mark.

"She's upset with your review," explained Nandita, frowning at Ria whispering to her father.

Alok came up to Nandita, looked at Saraiya and spoke rather heartily, with some sarcasm: "So this is the lady who feels that my intelligence has been assaulted by my wife's writing." He extended his hand, "Hello Saraiya I am Alok,

Nandita's husband."

Seeing Saraiya non-plussed, Shreela came up and nodded to Nandita. Turning to Sariaya, she asked, "Shall we leave, Saraiya? You have a flight to catch."

Sariaya turned to Nandita, "I'm sorry."

"For what?" asked Nandita.

"Last week."

It was Nandita's turn now. "I'm sorry too."

"For what?"

"For long ago."

They smiled at each other tearfully. Alok brought out a copy of the book from his jacket pocket and handed it to Nandita who presented it to Saraiya. She opened it to read the inscription:

"Tread Softly For You Tread On Dreams"

Kargil's Widows

The Sarpanch's wife was railing quietly at her husband. "Why did you have to bring them all here? To pollute our house like this? I'll have to wash everything, the whole house and call Maharajji for purification afterwards."

"*Oh ho, karai le je* (get it done). Stupid woman. You are worried about washing the house. Why don't you understand? Mantriji will come to our house... our house."

"And if he brings the ashes here, won't we have to perform all the ceremonies for the dead here too? Have you consulted Maharajji on that?"

For a moment the Sarpanch was non-plussed. He had never thought of that — death ceremonies, thirteen days of rituals and meals. He pushed aside the niggling worry. "They don't do all that. In any case, I'll take all the expenses from Madha. After all, it's for his son."

"Then send the ashes to his house."

"Why do you keep repeating yourself? If the ashes come here, Mantriji comes here — to my house — I am the Sarpanch."

"So?"

"What do you mean, So? It'll show all the villages around that I am the Sarpanch and Mantriji comes to my house."

"Stupid man. He'll make you spend and take a donation for his next election. The lady doctor told us there'll be another election soon."

"So what? Why don't you understand, woman — that Bholaram who is *mukhia* (leader) of the *Bhangis* wanted the ashes to go to his house. It is at the head of their lane. How could I tolerate that? We all would have had to go there or to Madha's hovel at the end of the lane — even Mantriji. How could he? Even with the ashes."

"He goes there willingly enough when he wants to collect votes. This visit is also for election purposes only. Not to see you, the village or its problems or Madha, you stupid oaf."

There was a macabre note to the festivity in the village; a festivity alien to Death and the sombre portrait on the flower-bedecked altar at the village chowk: the multi-coloured buntings and the welcome arch, all for the dead?

There had been no such welcome for the two live heroes — young jawans who came home to nurse their war wounds — one with a stump for an arm, the other with grievous wounds in the shoulder and leg. Both lived in the village over the hill.

The macabre festivity was reserved only for the dead hero; the whole village was in an uproar. Today Mantriji was bringing his ashes home. He had been dead six weeks, on a faraway rocky slope, torn apart by enemy shells.

How much was actually him in the urn of ashes? Did no-one wonder?

The story was told and retold —- of his valour in the face of the enemy, of his lost body, found after weeks, at least portions believed to be his, after the maggots had been at work. A birthmark on his cheek and stitches on his leg identified him, so they were told.

Remember, he had come home to recuperate from that accident which left those stitches? That was the last time he'd come home and Belliya still hugged his last secret inside her. She had not told anybody that she carried his seed in her.

Bhim, the dead hero used to live almost at the bottom of the crookedest lane of Nanavas. It wound right and left and around, so that if you stood at the head of the lane, at the narrow opening from the chowk, you could not see Bhim's house at all. Only if you walked down the crooked lane and it turned, then you could not miss it.

Bhim's house stood out from its neighbors' kutcha hovels; some had one or two pucca walls, some even half a pucca wall, but all the four walls of Bhim's house were brick ones. As a matter of fact, the stones for the flooring were stacked in a corner of the courtyard and the order had been placed for the mangalore tiles for the roof and for the cement. He was to complete all that on his next annual leave in September. This was June. Who would do it now?

The argument between the Sarpanch and his wife would have carried on much longer, but for sounds of arrival. It was the bus. It bore the grief-stricken father of the widowed Belliya. Atop his dhoti was an old coat adorned with his newly burnished medals; a generous military mustache bristled snow white. The old soldier did not stop to return any greeting. Heading straight to his destination, he took in the all-too-obvious festivity, the anticipation in the air, the welcome arch — all far away from his widowed daughter's home.

Prudently he curbed the sneer that almost rose to his lips. 'Scavengers. Living off the dead,' he thought. He covered his face with the tail of his turban as he stepped into the lane. Onlookers assumed that it was either the stink or to wipe his eyes.

His quick progress checked at the newly built doorstep of his *samdhi's* house. Madha was waiting for him. The underground telegraph had informed him within seconds of the soldier alighting from the bus. They exchanged formal, unsmiling greetings and condolences. One had lost a son, the other a son-in-law.

Suddenly a bundle of black assaulted the Old Soldier. Thin arms flailed at him, sobbing and ranting, "Baba, Baba, why me, why me? You promised that everything would be smooth sailing and peaceful. I believed you and see what has happened...."

After a brief moment's confusion, the Old Soldier took her flailing hands into his, holding her firmly close to muffle her voice along with her sobs in his shoulder. But before he could say anything, a posse of ghouls descended, surrounding his daughter, softly attempting to tear her away from him.

The black robed ladies of the household — her mother-in-law, sisters and aunts-in-law, other female relatives in traditional black clothes and the party workers in starched white saris. They spoke almost in unison. "Beta, you should be proud. He is our *shaheed* (martyr). He has done our village proud. He has given his life for his country."

They tried to prise Belliya away, only to unleash a fresh torrent. "Quiet," she was commanded harshly. "Stop this. How can you behave like this? Mantriji will be here anytime and the TV cameras will be with him. Are you going to show your tears on the TV?"

That mother of all platitudes was trotted out to silence her: that the widow of a martyr was not an inauspicious widow. She was the eternal '*suhagan*' (married lady).

The ringleader of the white saris, a regular battle-axe who till now had stood apart, lips pursed, stepped into the circle. She gripped Belliya with a vice like grip, voice dripping acid: "You must not spoil this show like this. If you cry like this, your eyes will be red and swollen. Have you thought of that? And I told you to wear a white sari."

Shocked into sudden silence, Belliya looked up bewildered. "White sari?"

"How will it look on TV, if you the widow are standing there, in these..." she floundered for adequate words. After some stuttering she got it out, "these black tatters?" She motioned disparagingly at the black skirt-blouse and barely oiled hair of the grief-stricken widow. It was not her words. It was the look, the gesture, which evoked a response.

It was the mother-in-law taking umbrage. "No white saris. We do not wear white saris. That is not our custom." The old crones with her concurred solemnly.

"Never mind that. We (emphasis was on the 'we') are all wearing white for her sake. She should wear it for our sake."

"Why? That is not our custom"

"Why don't you understand? It will look bad on TV. Everybody expects to see a widow in white. How can she be different? She is a soldier's widow."

The mother-in-law bristled and the other community elders turned towards the raised voices. "In our community, we wear these clothes — not white saris. If it looks bad on your TV, don't bring it. No Fauji sahib said anything about white saris."

"But it is Mantriji who is bringing the TV with him."

"We did not ask for your Mantriji or for his TV. You should have brought the ashes right here. Why are you taking them there?" Her face alive with despair and scorn, the old woman made a derisive gesture towards the head of the lane. "We cannot change our customs for your TV or your Mantriji."

Madha her husband came up. "Stop it, woman," he commanded and led her aside. "If you carry on like this, they'll not give us all the money." He almost shook her with his fierce whisper, "you've lost your son and you want to lose the money also." He berated her as a commotion broke out.

"Come on quickly, Mantri sahib has come. Madha, where is Madha? Come on, come on man, you can gossip later." Madha was snatched up rudely by someone who propelled him to the gate. "Bhim's wife, the widow, where is the widow?" They almost panicked as Belliya pressed herself even more closely into her father's shoulder.

The women tried to pull her away, but Belliya continued to resist and finally the Old Soldier forced them to desist.

"Let's go Beti," encouraged the father. "Come, you're a soldier's daughter and a soldier's widow. Don't let us down."

Once again those platitudes.

Holding her firmly by the shoulder, he turned her and propelled her along in the crowd, headed for the chowk. As he went along, he gently wiped her face and smoothed her rumpled hair.

"Baba," moaned Belliya softly, "you got me into this... this marriage. You know I did not want it." Her tirade was soft and low, only audible to her father. Around them the spectators thought the young widow was praying. "I wanted to marry my Uka. But you said he was unsteady, he was not able to hold any job for long, how could he keep me. You said a soldier would be more loving and trustworthy; he would look after me all my life ..." at this point her dirge would have risen to a crescendo.

Instinctively, the Old Soldier's arm tightened warningly around his daughter. He shushed her under his breath. "We'll talk about all that later, not in front of all these people. I have come to take you home."

That pacified Belliya, who was rather stupefied by the sea of humanity which had, by this time, engulfed them. Surging forward, it propelled them to the Sarpanch's house, where all the village elders were assembled. The Mantri Sahib stood, holding the urn in his hands awkwardly. It was covered with the mandatory red cloth. A string of slightly tired marigolds shone against the red of the cloth.

Belliya was mesmerized by the marigold-topped urn. 'My life, my whole life,' she thought, 'lost inside that urn? No, now I'll go back home, back with Baba, back to my Uka...' Her thoughts soared, as her mind conjured up her childhood sweetheart.

She would have almost broken into a smile, had she not been rudely jerked forward. The stern-faced matron of the white saris pulled her forward, slinging a sari around her shoulders, shrouding her in 'their' white sari, hissing,

"Don't cry now. Oh, these red-rimmed eyes on TV!"

As she progressed, the party workers had been questioning each other mutely. Suddenly, one moved forward to block the TV camera's spotlight. Before anyone could protest, Belliya was cut off expertly from her father and her in-laws and surrounded by white clad party workers. The party worker allowed himself to be shoved away from the camera's eye.

The Sarpanch and the Mantriji carefully placed their hands on her head, blessing her for the camera. Even the officers who brought Bhim home were hemmed in by the white crowd.

"Vande Mataram. Bolo vande.... Bhimrao amar rahe"

Slogans rent the air. The TV cameras whirred, picking up shots of the startled widow, shrouded in an alien white, surrounded by loyal "villagers" and the Mantriji saluting her.

Belliya looked anxiously into the crowd, trying to pick out her family but the lights of the TV cameras dazzled her. She lifted her hand and rubbed it across her eyes. It made a poignant picture, which was to move thousands to tears.

But Belliya? She was traumatized, by her sense of loss, her insecurity in the crowd, the claustrophobia of the crowds and the buntings all around and the raucous blare of the loudspeaker, droning out speech after speech. Her mind turned blank, her eyes glazed over and she would have tipped over, if two women flanking her had not caught her in time.

When she surfaced again, another speech was on. Someone was reeling off lists of figures. She tried to pay attention. "Jeevan bhai *panch hazaar*, Patel Samaj *dus hazaar*, Vankar samaj *dus hazaar*...." As the list grew, Belliya noted her father's face grow longer. After sometime, his trademark sneer appeared briefly, before he quickly covered it with the end of his turban.

Finally the Army Officer took the mike. He spoke in Hindi. Belliya could follow a little. Bhim had taught her all he knew during his last leave.

The Sahib recounted Bhim's devotion to duty and his bravery. He expressed tremendous satisfaction that the community was reaching out to help his widow in her time of need. That, he emphasized, would be in addition to what the government would give her as pension and gratuity etc.

At last it was over. The Mantriji and his TV left — with deep salutations to the martyr's immediate family. And then finally the focus did come to them.

The crowds melted away quickly, the slogan shouting party workers in their hired trucks, their leaders slamming their car doors and brakes.

Unsure of what to do next, the family turned to head

home. The Sarpanch was confabulating with the Officers. He called out to Madha. "Wait, there are formalities to be fulfilled."

Madha looked suspicious. He looked questioningly at his *samdhi*. After all he thought he is an ex-fauji. The two came up, shoulder to shoulder. "What formalities?"

The Officer spoke up, "We must get Mrs Bhim's signatures on this file."

"Why?"

The Sarpanch butted in. "Madha, be sensible. Belliya must open a bank account and sign the papers to claim pension and everything else, gratuity, provident fund, the money for the house, the children...." he reeled off the list, holding up fingers for each item, eyes gleaming greedily.

Madha turned around. Handing over the marigold topped urn to his wife, he motioned to the womenfolk, "You carry on. I'll finish this off."

"No, no," the Sarpanch remonstrated. "Belliya must remain. She has to sign."

"Why?"

"The government will only give the money to her, in her own bank account, with only her signature. Not yours, not mine."

The old man chewed on that information, disappointment writ large on his face.

Belliya and her father held back. They approached the

table. Cleared of all the martyrdom paraphernalia, it now held the Officers, their files and papers.

The father saluted and spoke up. "How long will this take? Can we not do this at Dhrol, my village? I have come to take Belliya home and the bus is due shortly."

His words struck panic in Madha and the Sarpanch. Intuitively the two tacitly joined forces, when earlier it was the two *samdhis* against the over-lordship of the Sarpanch.

"Why?" the question was very sharp.

But the Officer was milder. "Why do you want to take her?"

The Old Soldier preferred to address his mates:

"Sir, you know these women. Already the whispers have started — she ate up her husband. They'll make my Belliya's life hell. And I can't stay to protect her. I have to go back."

Madha and the Sarpanch butted in. "She's our daughter. We'll look after her." For good measure, the Sarpanch added, "She's the pride of our village. How dare anyone say any such thing to her? I'll pull out their tongues."

The sahibs merely asked, "Why don't you stay for a week or so; let things settle down?"

"Sir, Belliya is not my only Kargil daughter." Belliya's bowed head shot up. "Bhim is gone but my Parbatiya's husband, my other son-in-law is hanging between life and death. She needs us there, me, her mother, her sister. Who knows what will happen?" His voice trailed off brokenly.

The Officers' lips tightened. "You must go, I can see that. How serious is it?"

The two soldiers looked deeply into each other's eyes and the younger man got the message as if it had been spoken aloud.

"Your daughter must follow later. Her bank account has to be opened, otherwise everything will be terribly delayed."

Now things moved quickly. The signatures were taken. Madha and the Sarpanch exchanged quick significant looks. The latter pressed a chit into Madha's hands.

He looked at it blankly, "What?"

"The account for today's expenses. Now you can afford to pay me."

The soldiers' lips curled. An old party worker who had been watching from outside the compound wall spoke up.

"Sarpanchji, the function was the party's. Why don't you collect from the party, instead of your widowed daughter?"

The sarcasm evoked a roar of raucous laughter from the usual hangers-on loitering near the chowk. Madha flung the chit down and shepherded his party home.

Belliya upbraided her father. "Baba, you never mentioned Didi to me."

"Where was the time, in all this? All this drama for the dead, Mantriji, Sarpanchji, party workers, the whole village. No-one asks after the ones who still live."

Madha make the usual soothing noises, asking after the

other son-in-law.

"He is very serious. That is why he is still in the command hospital. We don't know if he will survive. Belliya's mother is there already."

They reached the house and Madha had the string cot brought out into the courtyard. As soon as the news went inside, the womenfolk emerged to convey condolences. Before everyone's shocked and sympathetic eyes, the Old Soldier's shoulders sagged, his eyes dampened and a dam burst. It was a veritable litany. They listened fascinated, Belliya hanging on to every word.

"I am the culprit. I am the one. I was the one who married both my girls to faujis. Belliya didn't want to. She resisted for days, but in the end, she listened to me. I said... I said to her that he would be a steady person. The army makes a person steady. Everything is regular — eating, drinking, working, playing, even the pay, it is all steady and regular. That becomes a habit. So that not only will you be provided for while he works, but even after retirement, he'll continue to work because work will have become a habit. And he'll continue to bring you money.

"Uka is a wild one; he will lead you a merry dance, from one day to the next, you won't know what he'll get up to. She listened to me, obeyed me and see what it's gotten her. Bhim is gone now, only Uka is left. He may be unsteady, but he will be there...."

The voice trailed off into thought. After a pause, he resumed, "With Parbatiya, it was different. She was always different. She wanted a fauji and she wanted Sampat. They were so happy together, even for that little while that they had together, always teasing, and laughing and talking. I used to see them and pray that one day my Belliya could be that easy with her Bhim too.

"Lord knows what Sampat told her about his station, Parbatiya decided she must see it. I told her she could not go; there was no place for her; he could get court-martialled for sneaking her in as he had not been allotted any married quarters yet, but…

"For Parbatiya, a military station had all the lure of a forbidden fairy land. She was its fairy, so how could a fairy remain away from fairyland? In her mind's eye, she could picture it all: the parade grounds with her Sampat marching smartly, the dining hall with Sampat downing huge meals, the mess with him drinking others under the table, the firing range with Sampat's bull's eye with each shot. How could he go wrong? He was her Sampat.

"She dreamt of going to the station and meeting his officers and their memsahibs; of accompanying him to the gala, as if she was also a memsahib."

Parbatiya heard all her father and father-in-law's warnings and mentally discounted them as she made her own quiet plans.

One moonless night, she slipped quietly out of the village and walked for hours to catch the early morning bus. She told the daughter-in-law of the tea-seller at the bus-stop to inform her people, if they came inquiring.

What an adventure! Parbatiya couldn't quite contain her excitement. It was her first bus ride alone, but she schooled herself to act like a veteran passenger. The butterflies in her tummy were kept firmly down. Her gaze fixed out of the window, watching the green trees of her hills melt into the green patchwork of fields below and then, the dusty treeless roads. The day grew hot and then hotter, but Parbatiya was shivering with excitement. How surprised Sampat would be! How thrilled!

The thought buoyed her spirits and she was able to ignore the many side-long glances and several advances from male passengers unused to a young woman travelling alone.

Parbatiya had little actual trouble reaching her destination. She wasn't really worried about home; rather, was confident that her message would have been delivered well in time to stave off acute panic.

Clutching Sampat's whereabouts on a scrap of paper on which she had laboriously copied out the address from his last letter home, she approached the sentry at an imposing looking gate. "Go down 200 yards, turn left, again left and then right another 500 yards."

Parbatiya nodded a grave thanks, wondering what 200

yards amounted to on this hard road. Her feet were tired and aching and she was thirsty; and now more than a little anxious to end her 'adventure'. Doubts of Sampat's possible reaction assailed her as she recalled his remark, 'Officers prepare everything in advance. They don't like surprises.'

It was absolutely right. Faujis don't like surprises. Delighted as he was to see his young wife, Parbatiya's appearance put Sampat in a quandary. The sentry at his unit had managed to alert him without others being involved, but what if the CO got wind of it, as he was bound to?

Sampat approached his subedar sahib and poured out his heart. "*Janabji*, she is innocent, a little foolish. She's come without telling anybody at home, only left a message with a friend; what to do with her now, until someone comes to fetch her?"

The subedar's whiskers quivered involuntarily.

"You're a lucky dog to have landed such a tigress. She came all this way for you and no-one dared to touch her along the way. Now take care of her." But after a stern look he offered to help, promising to speak to a colleague with quarters, whose wife had gone home for some time. "She can stay there for a few days."

Parbatiya was a hit with the whole station. All the ladies officers and jawans were thrilled at the "bhabhiji's" adventure. Sampat came in for much back-slapping and ribbing.

Innuendoes flew about on his sexual prowess — was

it his randiness which had brought his wife post-haste to his side? Comments threatened to become more and more explicit.

Sampat was greatly inhibited by the presence of his seniors and their families. His silence had Parbatiya worried. "Don't you like me anymore? Didn't you want me to come?" she asked anxiously, until he took a few days leave to take her back home, where his responses were sufficiently amorous to allay her fears and the anger of the elders at her escapade. That was the last she saw of him, until... until he came back in pieces.

The Old Soldier's voice broke. "They loved each other so much. And now? What an accursed father I am who wishes his young son-in-law dead as early as possible?"

The raw emotions roughened his breaking voice. The words stirred through the audience crowding the tiny courtyard, bursting into a loud questioning murmur. It was vocalized hesitatingly by Madha in a single word, "Why?"

The word was a bullet, shot full of question, nervousness and wonder.

"Madha, *mere bhai*, you have no idea of Sampat's condition. Parbatiya and his mother are both beside themselves. No legs, wounds in the stomach, chest and neck. Even if he escapes death, which no-one is sure of, not even the doctors, how'll he survive, what'll he do? Sampat was a proud hero. Let him remain so. Can he beg? He has told Parbatiya he does not want to live and the doctors are not sure he will survive. All I can think of is that if he has to go, let it be as quick as possible. But those military doctors move heaven and earth to save lives, not to lose them. If Sampat goes soon enough now, Parbatiya will get her compensation and pension quickly enough. I'll be able to get her married again as soon as possible.

"Once this political jamboree is over, who will remember Kargil and its martyrs? *kya* Kargil, *kaun* Fauji? Who knows if they'll give the money at all then or make us run from desk to desk for years. I know even some memsahibs had such problems for years. And they were memsahibs. What is my poor Parbatiya? If Sampat lingers on for some months, all this urgency will definitely evaporate. Then what?

"That is why I pray that God relieve Sampat and my Parbatiya soon. I'll get both the girls married together."

All the while Madha had listened intently. Now his face closed. His voice was taut. "If you want to, you can get Parbatiya married. But Belliya is ours."

Instinctively, his sons and brothers closed around, enveloping both Madha and Belliya sitting at her father's feet. The eyes of the two old men met and held fast. The father's eyes, which a few seconds before had dwelt lovingly on his daughter's bowed head, now turned steely, his face cold.

Madha's equally stern face was hard — was it a streak of greed?

"She's my daughter. What is her place here now? Let

her come home, we'll resettle her. Uka still waits for her. He told me so."

There was a touch of pleading as his daughter slipped her fingers into his.

But Madha was adamant. "No, Belliya remains. For all we know, she may be carrying Bhim's seed, my grandson who'll inherit everything. Besides, there's work here. Our lands and the new land the government has promised. Who'll work that land? Belliya will have to do it; who'll handle all the files and accounts and all that? Besides, if she married, they may take the land away...."

"Let them," the Old Soldier burst out, "has she not suffered enough that you pass a life sentence on her, to eke out life looking after land and a bank account?"

There was more that he wanted to say...'that you're wanting to lay your hands on the land and the money, that's why you won't let my daughter come home.'

But discretion, he decided, was the better part of valour. Already the cracks had appeared and the signs were ominous. The Sarpanch and the village bania (money-lender) were crowding behind Madha; and the village hoodlums, never far away from money and land, had appeared like magic to station themselves near the gate.

The bania spoke up "Faujibhai, Belliya belongs to this village now. We will look after her. I've told Madha not to worry about seed and fertilizers for the new land. As soon as he clears his old loan, I'll open a new account for Belliya's land. The tractor loan can be paid off easily now."

There was some sympathy in the eyes of the women as they gazed at Belliya's bowed head; each word emphasized her life sentence. Her mother-in-law was obviously torn: sympathy was writ large on her face, but the eyes were lit up, reflecting the naked greed in the circle of men, father-in-law, uncles and brothers-in-law, creditors, goons, village elders.

The Old Soldier looked around for the Officers. They were nowhere to be seen, undoubtedly being discreetly entertained well away from the savage court which had pronounced a life sentence for his Belliya.

"Madha," he pleaded, "you have daughters too. Let my daughter get some happiness. She has done her duty and will continue to do it towards you."

"This," came the clipped reply, "is her duty, to look after her family. Go in peace. If she has to marry, let it be to her Bhim's memory, or to his younger brother" (a little boy of 9?)

It was abundantly clear that the vultures would never let go of this prey, nay this feast inadvertently offered to them. Belliya looked up at her father. The expectancy had left her face. It was now sallow, her eyes lifeless.

"Go, Baba," she said protectively, "look after Parbatiya if you can, before the vultures get her also. Tell Uka I will meet him in the next life."

Her voice was loud and clear. It shot a flame of fury

through Madha and he would have raised his hand. His *samdhi's* look stopped him. The look was steadfast.

"You said Belliya was your daughter? What guarantee do I have that you'll look after her once my back is turned, with Bhim gone?"

There was a raucous bellow from outside. "Who'll kill the goose that lays the golden eggs?"

An old crone stood up. "Shame on all of you. You call yourselves men? We should call you pimps or vultures, living off a widow and her husband's blood money?"

The old woman's son shot forward to quieten her. She flung him away.

"Madha, you *Makhi choos* (greedy man), now what are you?"

A babble rose, everyone speaking their piece. In the hubbub, Belliya led her father into the house, conscious of the careful watch of the self-appointed bodyguards.

"Beti," the Old Soldier spoke under his breath, "I can get you away at night. I'll speak to the Officers...."

"No, Baba, no. They have tasted blood. How long can I hide from them, even at home? You think they'll let me live in peace with Uka? They'll kill him too. All the money has been apportioned already in their minds. It is up to me now to see how long and in what ways I can hold out, to secure my own future and let them dance after me.

"Thank you for making me learn to write. They'll not

be able to cheat me. I'll be able to put different signatures everywhere so that they'll have to dance after me. Let them...."

"Beti, try to understand, they may try...."

She did not let him voice his worst fears.

"No Baba. Madha will not harm me but he'll not let go also. He wants this money very badly. Go now, so that I can call you again when I need your support. Go and look after Parbatiya before the vultures get her too."

Belliya pushed her father away as if by pushing him, she was hurrying him into Parbatiya's home before it was too late for her too.

A Survivor's Tale

The still figure on the bed turned her face painfully to thc door as it snapped open. Chutki heard her mother's footsteps enter, a little heavy, almost dragging – tired.

Opening her eyes took some effort, but Chutki did so and spoke in her new slow, hoarse voice, "What happened, Ma?"

The mother, Divya, motioned with her hand – 'wait'. She first headed for the washroom, freshened up and came out drying her face.

"Beta, I know you want to know everything. Let Saloni and Sandeep Bhaiya come, then I will tell all of you together, ok."

Divya looked down at her daughter, compassion writ large on her face. Chutki's colour was still pale and her voice was only barely audible; but she spoke now, not those dumb silences and hoarse ranting of four names that had filled their ears in the first fortnight: Dhir, Dhimant, Naveen, Ujwal. Those names were now engraved in their collective consciousness.

"You know, it was the first time I saw a real court from inside," she smiled. "It is not much like the gleaming images on TV or movies; the premises are overcrowded, with tables of touts and lawyers who don't have offices; hordes of people walking about, as crowded as any bazaar, as noisy as any mall. I had to ask to find my way to the courtroom where the case was to be heard, an ancient building, up a wooden staircase with steps which were worn away with use, round the gallery to the courtroom in the very corner. Musty smells, paan stains on every wall, corridors packed with sweaty bodies and a courtroom full of rickety chairs, often their plastic cane unravelled and dangerous to sit on, uncomfortable benches, a huge table for the lawyers, two for the stenos and clerks, two wooden railing bound stands for the accused and the witnesses and then the tall railing behind which the judge was ensconced, high above it all, mistress of all she surveyed, perhaps poor fools seeking 'Justice?'

"The judge," Divya spun out her story for all it was worth, quailing inside over what was to come, "was a very dignified looking lady, stylish bun, minimal make-up; she seemed to be impartial." Again she looked at her audience.

Chutki motioned with her hand, "Yes, they were there, all four and their lawyers; and our lawyer, the Assistant Public Prosecutor (APP). Since today was the first day, nothing much actually happened."

As Divya looked around, the accused whispered amongst themselves. Their lawyers were smug. Divya's support system, her parents and siblings sat straight, glaring at the accused.

The lawyer had warned that courtroom procedures were full of tedium that had to be endured. The case came up for hearing late. The APP, Ms Shruti, updated the judge on the charges against the four young men — gang rape, attempted murder and causing grievous hurt. Charges were framed for gang rape under Section 376 G, attempted murder Section 307, causing grievous hurt Scction 320. The ring leader of the accused who had managed to secure bail, stood apart from his friends, impassive to the charges read out by the judge. Then they insisted, "Not guilty".

Ujwal said "She asked for it. We gave it to her," holding up a mobile.

Ms Shruti started briskly, presenting the results of the police investigation, the evidence recovered from the site and finally the medical report. The doctor confirmed gang rape, burn marks on legs, abdomen and between the breasts, signs of tight bandages on the wrists and legs and some mysterious infected chafing under her chin. One arm was fractured, the elbow smashed and a serious head injury.

When that was brought out, the accused looked at each other, question marks on their faces.

Nothing was recovered from under her nails; plenty from the nails of all the four men. Semen had been matched too. The doctor testified that some instrument had apparently been used as she was bleeding; there was serious internal damage, leaving question marks over future conception, if ever.

Much more had actually happened. It was over a month since Chutki had been traumatized, and hospitalized. She was still in bed, still withdrawn, one arm in plaster, head woozy and speech minimal. No one knew how she had those terrible scratches under her chin which still oozed, apart from the slow-to-heal internal injuries. She had not spoken, apart from those four names. Medical examination pinpointed gang rape.

But her family had been busy.

On Day One, Sandeep had come home late at night to find her unconscious on the doorstep. He rang the bell and carried her in, against her weak struggles, "Don't touch me, don't touch me." A doctor was summoned but recognizing the status — gang rape plus head injury, plus fractured arm, he advised immediate hospitalization to ensure speedy treatment as well as collection of evidence.

Chutki was, as if struck dumb. Medical evidence filled in most of the blanks. She only rattled off the names: Dhir, Dhimant, Naveen, Ujwal in a hoarse low voice totally unlike her own melodious one and then shut her mouth, unable to speak for days. It was left to Divya to seek advice from a lawyer and speak to the police, offering the names, apparently of the men responsible for Divya's condition. They were taken into custody. Investigations proved their guilt, but one of them, with high placed connections, managed to obtain bail soon after the medical investigations were completed.

It was the young people who took the lead. Saloni and Sandeep had rounded up their close friends and cousins who could be trusted.

"We have to do something..."

"What Saloni di? What, without making it worse for Chutki?"

Sandeep had only one burning thought, "I'll kill them all."

His mother retorted sharply, "You'll land in jail then. What good will that do Chutki? Think with your head. This is not the time for murder. It is time for shaming all of them and their families, extended families, friends, everybody. Making an example of them. Work on that."

Suddenly everyone sat up.

"Find out about their families. Take photographs, even of their cousins and classmates, friends and neighbours, their *subzi wala*, *dhobi*, garage *wala*. Let the whole world recognize them as sisters, mothers, sisters-in-law, and girlfriends of rapists. Shame them in their own families and communities.

The harshest punishment will be when a sister's engagement will be broken because of what they have done or a cousin sent home by her in-laws because of the rape."

She walked off, leaving the young brains to do their job.

Two days later, early morning saw shoppers and rival shopkeepers in a bazaar smirking at the famous sweetmeat shop that dominated the bazaar. Even customers who entered the shop grinned and asked to taste the latest variety, leaving the staff puzzled. What was going on?

"Chotu, find out why all those people across the road are laughing..." the boss ordered. Chotu crossed the road and mingled with the crowd; then looked back perplexed. Everything seemed to be in order. Why were people laughing? He asked the peon at the stationary shop.

"Can't you read your shop's new signboard? Instead of Bhalubhai Sweets it is now *Balatkari* Sweets." Chotu's mouth fell open; he wondered how he would tell that to the Boss … *Balatkari* Sweets?

People had been clicking on their mobiles. In no time, a couple of press photographers appeared as Chotu ran across to brief his boss about the new name. Too late – the photographers had taken their pictures and left. Soon the afternoon editions were on the street, selling like hot cakes; the next morning, the whole town knew about the connection between Bhalubhai sweets and Dhir the rapist. There were pictures not only of the shop with the tell-tale hoarding, but also those of his parents, his nubile sister, some cousins and even an unidentified former girlfriend saying she knew he would get up to no good for his attitude had always been 'perverted'.

'How did they get these pictures?' wondered the family, looking around for someone to blame.

The families of the other men smirked in satisfaction. Dhir was after all only a *halwai's* son. It had to happen to them. Dhir's extended family cracked down on his parents: "Is this what you taught your boys? Who will marry the girls now?"

But nothing was said to any of the four boys in police custody.

As soon as the medical examinations of the four men were over, they applied for bail. A few days later, Naveen's bail application was being heard when his brother nervously entered the court, holding a rolled-up paper. He held on to it until bail was granted and his father exited the courtroom to head for the police station to complete the formalities. Then he showed him the afternoon edition, with large displays of the notice board of a popular upmarket bookstore – large posters displaying 'The Family of a Rapist' with pictures of their entire extended family, with some of Naveen's former girlfriends, close friends, his tuition teachers, their local store owner and even the paan-seller at the street corner.

"Recognize these people," screamed the headlines.

Two down: two to go. Now the families were on the alert, but for what? From where? When? Naveen's father was a big wig, yet this?

Young people are brimful of ideas, are they not? What now? Facebook and Twitter were buzzing in the whole city and beyond on this delicious scandal, with live pictures.

The following week, one sultry afternoon saw a gang of giggling girls enter a building in a condominium complex noisily. The security guard looked on. They were all well -dressed. He would not dream of stopping them and getting hauled up by any of the residents. They took the lift up. He watched – 10th floor, yes there was a college going young lady up there.

The young ladies walked up the next two floors to the locked terrace landing. A hammer from one of their capacious bags broke open the lock giving them access to the terrace. They scouted for direction, looking for a place which would be visible from all the surrounding buildings in the complex, but not accessible from any of the balconies, so it could not be cut down easily. 'Hit them at home,' they giggled.

The rolled up banner was weighted down on the inside so it would not fly in the breeze. That would make it useless. It had to hang down so it was visible to all. Ropes attached to its outer ends were tied down to the pipes running just off the ground. They waited quietly, surveying the ground below

– waiting for six pm, when children and young mummies would troop downstairs for games and gossip. One of them held a brand new lock and key in her hand. As the deadline came closer, some quietly left the terrace and took the lift down to stand quietly in a corner.

As the first of the kids appeared, the thumbs up signal was given and the banner rolled down triumphantly displaying *"Balatkari Khandaan dekho"*, with pictures emblazoned of Dhimant and his family, young and old and the family store, followed by a question, 'Is this their real *dhanda* (business)?' with all its shameful connotations.

Quickly, they locked the terrace with the new lock and pocketed the keys. It would take the guards a while to hunt for the old keys and obtain permission to break the terrace lock. Meanwhile the whole society would have seen the banner which was already captured on mobile cameras by the girls downstairs, for next day's headlines. Why tomorrow? Whatsapp was immediate.

After the first two incidents, the rape had become a talking point. Now it would be drawing room conversation everywhere with the 'hoi polloi' too. Schools and colleges were holding special lectures teaching self-defense to young women, and debates; but more than that, what made the headlines was an incident in a mall.

Divya's niece and her friends had trailed two of Naveen's cousins to a restaurant in a mall. Some journalists were 'conveniently' present too.

When the steward appeared for the order, the niece was loud and clear, "Do you serve food to Rapists and their families here? I thought you ran a respectable restaurant."

The voice carried to all the neighboring tables and everyone stopped to listen. The manager came, lisping in embarrassment, "Madam...."

"Don't Madam me. Get rid of those people," she pointed her finger, "or else all the rest of us will leave. Do you want to eat with a Rapist family?" she asked her audience.

"Why harass them like this?" one asked.

"Are you related to them?"

"I don't know them from Adam. But the judgment has yet to come."

"So today you will break bread with the family because he has not been judged. Tomorrow you'll say he is in jail, why punish the family. Right?"

"Why not? It's only human."

"What about the one who suffered and still does? Have you spared her a thought? Bothered to express any sympathy, any human feeling, light a candle, offer a single flower or a word to her or her family? That she was gang-raped has already been proved. Does she not deserve any of your humanity?"

Cameras flashed in several mobiles; the Press too took photos and another incident was recorded. A wave was being generated – all young people at work with their own ideas .... 'Attend a high profile wedding and get someone to introduce you to Naveen's family and then say loudly – "Oh the family of Rapist Naveen?"

There was still Ujwal to go. Saloni advised, "Let's give it a rest. Let them die of the suspense of not knowing when and how they're going to be hit. We have to concentrate on the trial just now. Just keep doing things like the restaurant with the other families also ... gardens near their homes, weddings they attend, whatever possible. If we don't touch Ujwal just now, the others will turn against him suspecting betrayal; then we can tap him or his people, maybe? Getting people to speak up in court is more important than Ujwal now."

They had already touched base with a number of young people across the town in schools, colleges and coffee shops. Sources were being tapped, before the courtroom drama started.

For all its tag of Fast Track Court, movement remained slow. Each piece of evidence and each report was examined; questions raised pointedly about the absence of the Survivor and the absence of any material from her nails to indicate that she had put up a fight and scratched any of the men. Weeks went past in all that.

The defense lawyer was voluble:

"Your Honour, my clients have said that it was voluntary. She wanted it. She had come to the party for just that. That is why she did not scratch them; that is why her nails were clean. See how she is hiding her face now. There is no case that is why they are trying to defame the boys with all those stunts in the newspapers."

Ms Shruti placed her hand over Divya's. "That argument was expected. Get her ready to talk while I present our witnesses."

Divya gave a gentle nod. Ms Shruti stood up to call her witnesses. That day, there were a number of ladies in the court, identical dupattas tied over their faces, eyes covered with goggles. The one who was called, removed her goggles and dupatta to take the stand. After the oath preliminaries, she told the court:

"Two of them, Ujwal and Naveen studied with me in school. They used to tease girls mercilessly and embarrass us. When we were in Std 12, just before the Boards, they announced that they had 'fixed' one of the girls and that she would not appear for the exam. At first no one believed them; but afterwards not only did the girl miss her exam, but her family left town and we have never heard of her again. There were rumours, but no one knew what actually happened."

"Do you have proof?" hammered the defense lawyers.

"Only the knowledge that one of the best students of the class did not give the Board exams for no rhyme or reason, after they had boasted about it."

Two more such witnesses took the stand one by one,

one from school and a boy from college too. The face of the judge showed doubt.

The next witness was a girlfriend who testified bluntly, "I have heard with my ears Dhir boasting that they had ensured that Chutki would never be seen in public again. 'We've finished her', he said."

Fortunately for her, her evidence was corroborated by a coffee shop patron who had been present that night and who had heard the rapists talking cheerfully of how they had trapped her at the party and gang raped her in a guard's cabin. "They said she would never sleep with anyone else again." He glared at the accused.

A young lady who had attended the same party testified that she saw Chutki leaving with Naveen and the other three following them out.

The mother of each of the accused was called up, "Has your son told you about this?" The responses were incoherent sometimes and dismissive in one case.

The judge was looking pointedly at the APP. Ms Shruti gave the signal and four copies of the Gita were brought, each with the picture of the mother and sister of the accused on it. Each of the men were told to place their hands on the book with the picture. "That is your mother, your sister and the Bhagavad Gita. Can you say on oath that you did not commit rape?"

Three of them withdrew their hands, as if singed. Naveen

boldly nodded.

"Your Honour, it is almost closing time. May I present my star witness tomorrow morning?"

There was anticipation in the air. 'Star Witness'. The gang rape had, of course, been already established. The four accused identified and tagged by forensic investigations. The question now was: voluntary as the accused maintained or rape as claimed by the survivor's mother?

There was a buzz when court convened. Ms Shruti was running late and came scurrying into the court just before the Judge entered.

"Few minutes, Your Honour, the lift was busy. The witness has arrived and will be here in a few minutes.' The Judge nodded gravely, obviously making a shrewd guess about the identity and watched the four accused carefully.

A wheelchair rolled in the Star Witness.

"Your Honour, the Survivor will tell her story," announced Ms Shruti.

Chutki was pale and wan, struggling to breathe regularly. Her arm in a sling, her head sported a bandage but when she opened her mouth, the low hoarse voice was the strongest that Divya and her siblings had heard in a long time.

"May I tell you my story, Your Honour?" she asked, looking directly at the Judge, who was sitting forward looking at her. She nodded gravely.

"It was at a party in a friend's farmhouse. I had promised

to put in an appearance, so I went but wanted to leave quickly. Naveen," she looked directly at him, "tried to persuade me to stay. When I insisted on going, he said he'd come with me till the gate. His friends followed him." She paused to catch her breath, closing her eyes at the recollection.

"At the gate, they pushed me into the guard's room nearby and started to grab at my clothes. I screamed but the music was loud. They stripped off all my clothes and laughed when I sat down to cover myself with my knees and arms. There was a bed there. They picked me up and put me on it and tied my hands and feet to its four corners. There was a small TV there, playing a porn CD. They said, 'watch it and you'll be begging when we come back for you.' I kept pleading 'please don't do this,' but they just laughed. One of them saw a big dog collar in the corner of the room. They brought it and put it around my neck to tie it to the ropes of the bed so I could not reach the rope on my wrists with my mouth. The scratches from the spikes and studs on that collar cut my chin and infected it. See...." she put up her face to expose the infection below her chin to the Judge. *One mystery solved.*

"The lawyer has been asking why I had nothing in my nails. Because my hands were tied. How could I scratch them? They all scratched and bit me; those marks were on my body. They held candles in their hands and went around me singing Happy Birthday and dripped the hot candle wax on me, leaving these burn marks." *Another mystery solved.*

Her voice had become lower and absolutely dull and lifeless. "I don't know when they came back, after how long. They were all drunk. Dhir even vomited there." *Another mystery solved.* "They put something inside me that made my whole lower body shake. Then…then…." The voice stilled.

Ms Shruti came to her rescue, "So then, one by one they came to you, is that right?"

"Again and again. Till I started bleeding at the chin every time I moved my head and from my bottom. Then they untied me and one of them put a pair of shorts on me and a vest. My clothes were torn already. They put me in a car and when we reached my home, they…they…."

It was the Judge who asked "What did they do?"

There was a long pause as she struggled to speak out the final horror:

"They dragged me out of the car and threw me on the ground, banging my back and head. Then each of them picked up an arm or a leg, swung me a couple of times and then flung me at the door handle hoping I would die when I fell down. I didn't."

The final mysteries solved — the head injury and the arm fractures from that banging against the door handle and falling on the hard floor from those violent throws.

It was not only the Judge who sat back stunned, eyes fixed on the trembling young woman in the witness stand.

Mother, sister, brother, grandparents, relatives and friends divided horrified gazes between Chutki and the four accused.

Their relatives were conveniently absent that day – until Naveen's brother shot into the court, waving a piece of paper which he handed to his lawyer, who declared, "Your Honour, she has taken her revenge already."

The Judge turned to the lawyer.

"The day after he got bail, the victim called Naveen on his mobile to meet her at the farmhouse, offering a compromise. When he reached there, she called him into a room and knocked him unconscious. When he woke up, she was gone and he was in pain. This is the medical report — a complete vasectomy was performed on him; he is only 24 but cannot have any children."

"Proof?"

"She called him to the same farmhouse."

Ms Shruti conferred with Divya and turned to the Judge.

"Your Honour, these rapists had taken away her mobile. It is with one of them or their families. Who placed that call? Perhaps one of Naveen's jilted girlfriends? How could the victim have rendered Navneen unconscious? She can barely stand, her arm is in a sling. What compromise option is there in this case? There is not a single girl in this city who will marry anyone of these..." she made a derisive gesture towards the four accused, "these rapists."

Divya and her parents were staring pointedly at the other

three, Dhir, Dhimant and Ujwal, looking them in the eye, down their bodies and then Naveen's. Menace was manifest in those looks, evoking unease bordering on terror in the guilty trio as Ms Shruti questioned Naveen:

"How do you know who called?"

"I recognized her voice."

"So the name did not appear on your mobile."

"No."

"When you did not know her well enough to have saved her number in your mobile, how did you recognize her voice?"

"I heard her speak and knew it."

"How?" turning to the judge, Ms Shruti explained, "Ever since that day, this young woman has barely spoken. When she communicates with her mother, it is either with her eyes or her hands. Today is the first time that we have heard her story. And her family can barely recognize her hoarse voice for her original one." Divya handed her a mobile tuned to a voice recorder. Ms Shruti sought the permission of the court and pressed play. Everyone heard a melodious singing voice hardly recognizable as the voice heard shortly earlier in the court.

Snapping it shut, Ms Shruti turned to Naveen, "So you still insist that she rang you up and knocked you unconscious. Does that medical report describe your head injury also? Or only a vasectomy?" she held out her hand for the medical report.

This time the doubtful look of the Judge was for Naveen.

The defense lawyer jumped up, "Why would he go in for such a vasectomy himself?"

"I did not say he did it himself; I only suggested a jilted girlfriend."

Naveen aimed a murderous look at his lawyer.

"Who's done it?" screamed the headlines. In due course, the judgment was pronounced – the condition of the Survivor made leniency redundant — life sentences were handed down.

"We will appeal," yelled all the families, but meanwhile the young men were locked away.

Divya moved away with her threesome. New city, new environment and new people did wonders for Chutki and her recovery. Divya devoted herself to her almost fulltime and the others chipped in to steer her. The day Chutki appeared for her UPSC exam, at the dinner table, she asked:

"See, I'm absolutely fine. Even appeared for UPSC. Now tell me, who did it?"

The family looked at each other. "Who neutered Naveen?"

Divya laughed. "Are you feeling guilty? I'm not."

"Who said anything about guilt? I want to know how it was done. It maybe needed by someone else some other time."

"Anytime Chutki. At your service," said Sandeep jovially. "By then, the medic would have become an expert at it."

"Tell me please." Sandeep and Divya looked at each other. The mother spoke: "Chutki, I called Naveen. You know how similar our voices are on the phone. I impersonated you at the farmhouse, in jeans, top and cap, standing near your bike, then running inside as his car stopped. He could not make out the difference – perhaps because he was expecting it to be you.

"Then, Sandeep and the medic took charge with chloroform to put him out, a quick slit and sutures. We were out of there in half an hour, stopped to take off the fake number plate so the farmhouse chowkidar's record would show a wrong number. Sandeep dropped me home and then the medic at the railway station. And that was it."

"Suppose the medic tells, Ma?" asked an awed Chutki.

"Would you tell if you did something like that for a friend of mine, Ms IFS-to-be?" asked Saloni.

The question hung over the table as they all looked at each other.